THE BURAQ PROJECT

MJ JAVANI

The Buraq Project is a work of fiction. The people and events depicted in this story are a product of the author's imagination. Any resemblance to actual events, or persons, living or dead is purely coincidental.

Published by:

UNIT 81 PUBLISHING

United States of America

E-book ISBN: 978-1-7330093-0-0
Print book ISBN: 978-1-7330093-1-7
Learn more about the author at www.mj-javani.com

CONTENTS

9-30-20

Dear Don,

Thank you for your interest and support. I hope you enjoy

this story!

All the Best!!

MJ Javani

DEDICATED TO

My father, who piqued my love of history and international affairs

Jill Javani, my first line reviewer, best friend and soul mate

A true hero, my cousin Hormozd, whose beautiful soul and bravery in the face of insurmountable odds inspired me to never give up

1. YILDIZ PARK, ISTANBUL, TURKEY

October 10

I *t's a perfect day for revenge.* Janusz Soltani scanned the surroundings as he watched Hamid walk slowly toward him down the tree-lined pebbled path. He was ready to give the head of Hezbollah's External Security Organization (ESO) his just reward. Timing was the only remaining factor. He must not open his fist too early. The park was vacant, as expected early on a Friday morning. If everything went according to plan, the head of the ESO would be oblivious to his fate. As far as Hamid knew, Janusz was his Iranian Islamic Revolutionary Guard Corps (IRGC) contact.

The sun beat down as Janusz opened the top button of his dress shirt. He used the handkerchief in his pocket to wipe the sweat off his forehead and eyebrows. To his surprise, the air was filled with a sweet fragrance. It must have been the jasmine flowers that grew in abundance around him. The park was filled with trees neatly trimmed to perfection.

Overhead, the pillow-like clouds cast strange shadows on the ground, and the black-feathered crows danced on the air currents while singing an ominous song. Was nature trying to warn him? There was no use in pondering such thoughts. He took a seat on a wooden bench off the path. Hamid was getting closer. Janusz pretended not to notice. His body tensed as Hamid took the seat next to him.

"*Salam Aleikom*, my brother," the ESO chief blurted out.

"*Aleikom al Salam*," Janusz said.

Hamid swiftly launched into fluent Farsi. "Where does the path to Jerusalem begin?"

"The path to Jerusalem begins in Karbala."

With this reply, Hamid's face grew visibly relaxed. He tried to lighten the mood. "They tell me you're an expert in martial arts, that you kill most men with your bare hands."

"People say lots of things, brother. I've heard it said that you murder women and children. We should not believe every-thing we hear."

At a loss for words, the ESO chief raised both eyebrows slightly and let out a weak laugh. "Hezbollah has been under tre-mendous financial pressure lately. The cash infusion from the IRGC is our only lifeline these days," Hamid said.

"It hasn't been a walk in the park for us either. The latest round of US sanctions has slashed our budget."

"Praise be to Allah for Ayatollah Mashhadi and the IRGC. If not for them, where would we be?" Hamid said.

Janusz stole a furtive glance around the park. They were still alone. "Tell me something, Hamid. Do you enjoy killing Americans?" Judging by his face, the chief of the ESO didn't know what to say. He probably assumed Janusz was testing him.

"I don't know if 'enjoy' is the right word, brother. It's an honor to kill the infidels who've invaded our land. Wouldn't you agree?" Hamid said.

"Invade. I guess that's one way to view it. Another way is to accept that we leave them no choice when we kill civilians in Rome or New York."

Hamid stared at Janusz with furrowed brows, his upper lip twitching ever so slightly. "You're a funny man. I must admit the war in Syria and the long drive to Istanbul have worn down my sense of humor. Let's leave the jokes for our next meeting." After a short pause, Hamid got straight to the point. "When can I get the five million dollars the IRGC promised us?"

"Who said anything about a joke? My dear Hamid, you're here so I can kill you. I blame you for planning the attack that killed my brother back in 1995."

Hamid's face turned red. They stared coldly into each other's eyes. The first man to blink at a moment like this is always the first to lose. Then it happened, a bead of sweat rolled down Hamid's forehead. His hand was shaking as it moved toward his hip. Janusz struck the side of Hamid's face without warning. The move startled the ESO chief, who let out a mild grunt. Janusz then pricked his opponent with a small needle. Hamid responded with a childish taunt.

"Is this supposed to hurt me?"

"The needle is laced with a powerful poison. You'll be dead within the hour," Janusz said.

"You American dog! I'm going to kill you," Hamid shouted, before lunging at him. The force of the impact threw Janusz to the ground. He grabbed his opponent's waist, pulling Hamid down with him. The two men rolled ceaselessly on the ground. The stones of the pebble path dug into Janusz's back each time he was on the bottom. They finally came to a stop in a soft, wet patch of grass.

"You pig. I'm going to fuck your mother."

"Hamid, your insults are beginning to bore me."

Janusz's taunt had the intended effect. Hamid flew into a fit of rage, swinging his fists at the American with no particular aim. Janusz skillfully moved to mount his chest for a more targeted response. The first punch came as a shock to Hamid. The third visibly broke his nose. The fifth knocked the wind out of him. Janusz brought his face close and peered into Hamid's eyes.

"How does it feel to know you're going to die?" Janusz said.

"Not as bad as knowing that Hezbollah will rape your sister." Hamid struggled to break free of the American once again. He moaned and groaned and pushed as hard as he could. It was no use. The American was too strong. As the realization set in that there was no escaping his fate, Hamid showed visible signs of panic. No longer concerned about Janusz, he searched for a way out. Hamid slithered on the ground like a snake as

Janusz sat on his chest. The sweat pouring down Hamid's fore-head soaked his eyebrows and beard. His breathing grew louder as his heart pounded. A minute later, everything calmed down. Hamid's heart was no longer pounding. The poison was working faster than expected. Janusz stood and shook himself off. A wave of happiness washed over him.

Before he could savor the moment, voices approached in the distance. They were speaking Turkish. His suspicion was immediately confirmed. There were two police officers in black uniforms coming toward him. One was talking into a wireless device. Out of the frying pan and into the fire. They must have been at least a hundred feet away. There was no good explanation for why Janusz was standing over a dying man who had been punched in the face one too many times. His legs made the decision faster than his mind. Before he knew where he was going, Janusz ran at full speed through the park. He didn't bother to turn back, assuming the cops were in hot pursuit. Groups of pedestrians were now strolling about. One by one, they stopped to stare as he raced by.

He prayed no one would try to help the police by blocking his path. As he turned around a tree to change direction, Janusz maneuvered straight into the path of a young couple oblivious to the unfolding commotion. He knocked down the woman as her male companion stood frozen. The woman flew several feet in the air before landing on her back. As soon as she shook her head, he hoped for the best and resumed his escape. Her male companion started chasing Janusz long enough for the police to catch up.

The park was separated from the street by a stone wall covered with overhanging branches. Janusz sprinted toward the wall, grabbing onto a thick branch. He pulled himself up in one motion. A second later, he was on the other side. A quick glance revealed the police were no longer behind him. He ran down the street as fast as he could toward a nearby intersection. A taxi was waiting at a red light. As he grabbed the door handle, the light turned green. Janusz was already inside.

The driver turned to shout in Turkish at his unwelcome customer.

"Take me to the Sheraton," Janusz said wiping the sweat out of his eyes. A slew of protests followed.

"The Sheraton!" Janusz said more emphatically.

The taxi was now blocking the intersection. A chorus of honks ushered forth raucously from behind.

"Sir, I'm on lunch. Please get out!" the driver said.

Janusz pulled out a wad of cash and waved it in front of the driver's face.

"The Sheraton, let's go."

"Close the door," the driver said.

Off they went toward the highway. Half an hour later, they arrived at the Sheraton, Istanbul. Janusz paid three times the normal fare. When the cab was out of sight, he walked across the street to the Istanbul Oriental Hotel. Inside his room, Janusz took a warm shower before changing clothes. He imbibed several tiny bottles of alcohol from the minibar to help take the edge off. If they had not found him by now, the Turkish authorities had lost the trail. He needed to clear his head. He grabbed a chocolate bar before heading out to a nearby park overlooking the Bosporus.

As he gazed out at the waterway separating Asia from Europe, it finally sunk in that Hamid Ajami, the mastermind behind the murder of his brother, was dead. A cool breeze drifted off the water and hit his face. The afternoon sun was blinding.

All around, the horizon evoked a distant connection to this place. Perhaps it was the realization that his great ancestors, the ancient Persians, had once crossed this body of water to conquer the troublesome Greeks. Innumerable boats made their way to and fro on the blue waters. As he stared at a ship in the distance, Janusz was satisfied with his mission. It was time to return and brief his colleagues in Virginia.

2. HIGH RISK CAPITAL HEAD-
QUARTERS, HERNDON, VA

October 11

High Risk Capital (HRC) LLC occupied an ordinary office building in the suburban Northern Virginia community of Herndon. Located in the heart of the Dulles Technology Corridor, off the Dulles Toll Road, Herndon was the home of numerous defense-related technology firms that depended on the Pentagon for their prosperity. HRC was different from its neighbors in many ways. Most notably, the company was a private equity firm that specialized in buying and selling small to medium-sized businesses, and all of its acquisitions were located outside North America.

Most of HRC's competitors in the private equity world maintained their offices in New York City or Washington, D.C., but the founders of HRC understood that locating their headquarters in Herndon would serve them well. Ten years earlier, the company had acquired a six-story, glass-encased high rise for its headquarters. The external facade of HRC's building was surrounded by black-tinted glass on all sides, reflecting only the immediate surroundings of trees and parking lots to the outside observer. Inside, the lobby was more ornate than similar buildings in the office parks of Northern Virginia. All floors were covered with white Italian marble to convey the right message to clients from far away countries in the Middle East, Asia, and Africa. Foreign investors usually expected such extravagance from their business partners in the private equity world. The senior partners at HRC had decided early on that each floor in the six-story building would focus on a different region of the world. The Middle East offices were located on the first floor, Africa on the second, Asia on the third. The offices of the corporate executives along with state-of-the-art conference rooms were located on the top floor.

Once inside his first-floor office, Janusz reflected on the events in Istanbul. Killing was not something he relished, but Hamid Ajami was no ordinary man. He was planning to kill Americans. In an age of moral relativism, Janusz was defending a set of principles. Amongst these was doing whatever necessary to protect his country from those wishing to do her harm. That was hard for the bureaucrats in Washington to understand but not for Janusz. Whenever he needed a reminder of his chosen path, he read the framed article from his student days at the University of Virginia. It was an excerpt from an interview he had provided to Vanessa, a reporter from *The Cavalier Daily*:

> *Our featured guest, Janusz Soltani, majors in economics. He organizes fundraisers for children with cancer. Besides English, he is fluent in Polish, Russian, Persian, and Arabic. Below is an edited version of my interview with Janusz Soltani.*

> *Vanessa: Mr. Soltani, please tell us a bit about your family background so our readers can get a better sense of who you are.*

> *Janusz: Well, both my parents are UVA Alumni. My father, Farhad Soltani, came to the US from Iran in the early 1970s to study medicine at the UVA Medical School. My mother, Paulina Zielinska, arrived in the US from Poland as a child. She studied economics as an undergraduate at UVA where she met my father, the dashing medical student from Iran. They got married shortly thereafter. My father originally planned to move the family back to Iran after finishing his training, but all of that changed with the Islamic Revolution of 1979. Our family*

was secular, which put them on a collision course with the new Islamic authorities.

While we're on this subject, I want to take a minute to talk about my brother, Benjamin Soltani. Ben was just 14 years old when he was murdered on a school trip to Rome in 1995. The Iranian regime was after an opposition figure, whom they had tricked into showing up at a popular café, not too far from the Trevi Fountain. In order to get their man, the Hezbollah hit team, working on behalf of Iran, placed a powerful explosive inside the café. The blast killed eighteen people altogether. Unfortunately, my brother and a few of his friends had stopped at this café for ice cream. The explosion instantaneously turned my brother, his friends, and a few of the other patrons into dust. There wasn't much left of . . . excuse me . . . it still weighs on me.

  Vanessa: Take your time.

Janusz: There wasn't much left of his body to send back home. This tragedy severely traumatized our family; my parents and I are still struggling to cope. I sometimes wake in the middle of the night screaming. I don't want my brother's death to be for nothing. It is my sincerest wish to bring the perpetrators to justice one day.

Vanessa: I am very sorry for your loss. Let's try to switch gears a bit. Who do you consider a hero?

Janusz: Besides my brother who died way too young, I have to say that my heroes are my parents. They were both immigrants to this country, and they both became successful. This is especially true in the case of my father who came to America as an adult. Most of his family was in Iran before 1979, which made it harder for him to adjust. I give him credit for staying here after the revolution to give me the opportunity to grow up in a safe environment where I could enjoy freedom. Given this his-

tory, family is very important to me.

Vanessa: Is there anything else you want to tell our readers?

Janusz: Yes, I just want to say that I cherish the constitutional protection of individual freedom. Fortunately, the Polish side of my family has been able to enjoy freedom since the fall of the Iron Curtain. However, the Iranian Government continues to brutalize its own people while exporting terrorism abroad. It's my hope to one day help bring an end to that regime.

After reading the interview once more, Janusz made his way to the meeting with the heads of HRC. It was on the sixth floor where the office of HRC's CEO, Tony Volpe, was located. He had a corner room overlooking the back of the building with views of Dulles Toll Road. At nine in the morning, the executive floor was abuzz with activity to acquire a trading company in Dubai named Rostami Partners. Tony had explained that a presence in Dubai was critical to conduct business with every country in the Middle East. More importantly, they would gain access to the populous Iranian market.

A small group had gathered in the conference room to review the final details of the acquisition. HRC's vice president, Stan Roth, expressed concerns that Rostami Partners' executives had contact with the IRGC. Stan explained that conducting business with these men might cause problems with the US government executive departments and agencies, including Treasury, Commerce, and possibly even the IRS.

"Tony, we've been over this a dozen times," Stan explained. "I just think that the heartburn we'll get from the regulatory agencies won't be worth the potential profits. Besides, reports indicate the principals at Rostami have connections to the Iranian security services." Stan had been a bond trader with Solomon Brothers before the first attack on the World Trade Center in 1993. He had joined HRC as an expert on investments in developing countries after the attack.

"That's beside the point, Stan," Tony insisted, smoothing his blazer. Unlike Stan, who wore off-the-rack Macy's suits, Tony only bought, almost collected, fine garments. "You have to consider this acquisition from a long-term perspective," he continued. "There are powerful financial interests in this country that are lobbying our government to reestablish relations with Iran. It's only a matter of time until an administration comes along that will take our country down this path." Tony stopped for a sip of water, "With Rostami Partners, we'll have a presence there before our competitors. We can replace the management at a later time. The company's connections will come in handy at the right moment. Janusz, what do you think?"

Janusz Soltani, the youngest man in the room, was still suffering the pain of jet lag and was in no mood to talk. However, he was the principal analyst on the Middle East, and his opinion was sought in these matters. Toned and strong, he had what most considered a handsome face. His ability to blend in anywhere he traveled was the most remarkable aspect of his features. His skin could shift from fair to olive depending on his exposure to the sun. His eyes and hair appeared natural, no matter what color he chose to give them. These characteristics were invaluable to his work.

"My research indicates that Rostami Partners makes its profits by acquiring sanctioned Western goods popular in Iran. The company then sells what it legally buys from the West to dummy corporations set up by the Iranian Revolutionary Guards. The IRGC transports these goods to Iran and distributes them to licensed dealers at a higher markup. Acquisition of Rostami Partners will give us the access we seek."

The room was silent as the other participants pondered the implications of Janusz's assessment.

"Janusz is right. Despite the initial inconveniences, it will be a good long-term investment. Let's close this deal," Tony said.

Tony turned to Janusz, who immediately activated the

conference room phone. He made the call to Dubai with the others listening in. The bulk of the conversation was conducted in Farsi, which Janusz had perfected over many years of practice.

"Gentlemen, I believe we have a deal. Mr. Rostami is ready to shake hands. He wants to meet in Dubai to sign the contract," Janusz said.

"Okay, we've got some work to do. Let's make this happen," Tony said.

Janusz was certain Rostami Partners would make it easier for HRC to operate in the Persian Gulf, especially on the Iranian side. HRC had sought access to Iran since its formation in 1981. In fact, Tony had hatched the plan to create a private equity firm as a cover for the Unit's activities.

Unit 81, known internally as the Unit, was the unofficial name of a privately funded intelligence organization that had been created in response to the failure of the US Intelligence Community (IC) to predict the Iranian Revolution. As if that wasn't bad enough, the United States had been unable to plan the successful rescue of its hostages taken by the Islamic revolutionaries. In 1980, the mission to rescue the American hostages in Tehran had ended in a spectacular failure. Eight American commandos had perished in the Iranian desert.

Many in the IC, including Tony, believed these deaths could have been prevented if the congressional committees of the 1970s had not gutted the covert action capabilities of the CIA. Tony was fed up. After the National Security Council (NSC) rejected his hostage rescue plan, he'd decided to resign from the CIA to join his cousins on Wall Street. A few weeks later, however, he'd been inspired by an idea. Tony wanted to bring together a select group of former intelligence officers and patriotic Wall Street investors to create a private intelligence agency that would not be bound by the same oversight requirements that impeded the effectiveness of the CIA. Specifically, the group would be dedicated to carrying out the type of non-attributable covert operations that were originally assigned to the CIA. The Unit's primary duty would be to neutralize the greatest threats facing the nation. They would not waste resources collecting or analyzing intelligence for policymakers. That function was better left to the official intelligence bureaucracy.

The problem was that the CIA was an instrument of executive power. This meant that anytime congress and the president were at odds, the Agency's operations were subject to selective leaks by the congressional intelligence oversight committees. This dilemma was further exacerbated when the executive power was in the hands of one party and the congress in the hands of the other. The security of the nation had become hostage to party politics.

Preventing this harmful government fratricide was how Tony had sold the idea of the Unit to his contacts in New York back in 1981. Despite the investors' eagerness for the project, there had been many obstacles to overcome, especially that of funding. The need to finance the Unit's activities had been addressed with Tony's proposal to create a private equity firm as a cover. The front company had eventually taken the name High Risk Capital. The group had planned for its employees to become proficient in both financial matters and intelligence operations. HRC was to become proficient in corporate valuations, arbitrage, hedging, and commodities trading. With an initial investment of fifty million dollars, the new company had begun to fund its covert operations through investment activities.

Another obstacle was finding ways for the new organization to de-conflict its activities with those of the US government. It would be necessary to inform select members of the US government about the activities of the Unit to prevent concurrent operations against the same target. If that problem weren't solved, the Unit would itself become the target of US intelligence.

Inviting senate leaders from both parties to exploratory meetings in New York, early in 1981, had solved the problem with de-confliction. Tony and the investors were pleasantly surprised when the senators had agreed that there was a need for an organization that would address a limited number of the nation's most pressing national security challenges. The politicians had been ecstatic that the government would not have to fund these activities. The arrangement allowed them to honestly deny knowledge of the Unit's operations. What's more, the US government could take credit for any spectacular successes by claiming the victory for the CIA. It was the best of all worlds for the politicians. It had been decided that the Unit would coordinate its activities with the Senate Select Committee on Intelligence, or SSCI. The committee members had taken an oath to never reveal the Unit's activities at the risk of having that capability disappear. Their job was to ensure that there would be no conflict with the official intelligence bureaucracy.

Furthermore, during the course of their intelligence oversight activities, the senators had the option of handing over to the Unit any operation that the CIA was hesitant to tackle. The senior SSCI staffers would meet twice a month with members of the Unit to inform them of the most imminent national security threats that had been brought to their attention. The SSCI would then defer to the Unit regarding which threats it was best able to tackle, given its resources.

Once the additional details were hammered out, a verbal agreement was finalized for the senators in 1981. The Executive Branch would not be consulted because the president might consider the activities of the Unit as a threat to his executive authority. The senators agreed to keep the Executive Branch out of the Unit's way when necessary. They also promised that if one of them ever became president, he or she would ignore the Unit's activities. Since then, each time the committee had been assigned new members, they were immediately briefed about the Unit and sworn to secrecy.

A few weeks after the agreement had been finalized, Tony incorporated HRC as a Delaware company. He decided that the most appropriate name for the new organization was Unit 81, the year of incorporation. Shortly thereafter, members of the group began referring to themselves as the Unit. If there had been any initial doubts about the potential for success, those doubts were laid to rest within a relatively short time. In the 80s, there were stories about Hezbollah operatives who disappeared. In the 90s, Russian nuclear scientists working for unsavory regimes died under mysterious circumstances.

Everyone assumed such deeds were the work of the CIA, and the Agency didn't mind taking credit for them. This, in turn, made it easy for the Unit to continue its operations. After reviewing the details for several more hours, Janusz was convinced that acquiring Rostami Partners was a good move. His mind was now completely numb. It was time to visit his parents.

Janusz veered to the right shoulder directly from the fast lane. He put on his hazard lights and grabbed his cell phone. He reviewed the scores as fast as he could. In the NBA, the Lakers had lost again, but Golden State was victorious. For some odd reason, the Celtics had lost to the Bulls, but the Suns had beaten the Mavericks. On he went to the NFL. The Redskins, the local team that could never get its act together, had pulled out a miracle against the Patriots. The news was not much better in the boxing world. All in all, only twenty percent of his picks had come through. He was out at least eight hundred dollars. There was always next week, and dinner was waiting.

3. SOLTANI FAMILY HOME, MCLEAN, VA

October 11

He walked up the front lawn and took a deep breath. The scent of Persian food permeated the air as Janusz rang the doorbell at his parents' house in McLean, VA. His mother, Paulina, had prepared his favorite dish, Ghormeh Sabzi, a traditional Iranian dish of vegetable beef stew served over a plate of white rice. She had taken the time to learn all the Iranian dishes in addition to the cuisines from her native Poland. After dinner, they sat in the living room for dessert and conversation.

The Washington Times had featured an article that morning about American foreign policy in the Middle East. Specifically, the role of the CIA had piqued his father's interest. Farhad asked his son why this legendary agency always got involved in conflicts that turned the people of the Middle East against the United States.

Janusz explained that the CIA was an instrument of the US Executive Branch. It didn't make policy; it only carried out what was asked of it. He answered his father's inquiry by recounting the history of American intelligence activities. Janusz explained that the National Security Act of 1947 created the Central Intelligence Agency. This congressional act was passed to centralize the collection and analysis of strategic intelligence for US policymakers, especially the president. The CIA was deemed necessary in the aftermath of the Pearl Harbor

disaster on December 7, 1941. The United States had traditionally avoided keeping a large intelligence apparatus due to fears
that the Republic would become a police state. Americans had
historically feared a strong federal government more than a potential foreign invader.

Before World War II, foreign intelligence collection and
analysis had been an uncoordinated activity between the Federal Bureau of Investigation (FBI), the Office of Naval Intelligence (ONI), and the Military Intelligence Division (MID). In
the past, there had been little cooperation and coordination
between these organizations, and the country had paid a high
price in Pearl Harbor. To meet the needs of a centralized foreign intelligence service, the United States had created the
Office of Strategic Services (OSS) in 1942 to collect and analyze
foreign intelligence for the Executive Branch. Janusz explained
that it was during this time when American policymakers first
realized that a centralized national intelligence service could
provide a capability for senior policymakers to date unavail-
able from the FBI, ONI, and MID. The OSS first learned to conduct
"special activities," such as sabotage and psychological operations, from the British during World War II.

Over time, these special activities, later called Covert Actions, became the primary source of America's foreign policy
blunders during the Cold War. Influential circles in Washington felt that these special activities had played a useful role in
frustrating the Nazi war effort during World War II. Therefore,
a National Security Council document, referred to as NSC 10/2
retained the activities as tasks that would be assigned to the
CIA. Post-war policymakers argued that these activities were a
legitimate tool that could serve a similar function against the
Soviet Union and its proxies around the globe. The trick was
that the activities in question needed to be both deniable and
nonattributable to the US Government.

By the time such activities were called Covert Actions,
the CIA had developed a variety of capabilities to destabilize
regimes deemed to be amenable to Soviet influence. The most

successful acknowledged Covert Action to date was Operation TPAJAX, the effort to help the Shah of Iran consolidate his power in 1953. There was also Operation PBSUCCESS, the overthrow of Jacobo Arbenz in Guatemala in 1954. In the 1960s, the bulk of Covert Actions were conducted against Soviet proxies in Southeast Asia. The 1970s witnessed the disenchantment of the US population with the Vietnam War. There were accusations that the CIA had spied on American citizens opposed to the conflict. Numerous congressional inquiries of CIA operations caused a backlash against Covert Actions in support of unsavory regimes. The uproar was the impetus for congressional oversight of the CIA, decimating its Covert Action capabilities.

Janusz had learned that many specialists in foreign propaganda and psychological operations were fired. A few were redirected to other parts of the Agency. Things got so bad that, by 1979, the CIA was no longer able to predict the Iranian Revolution or plan to rescue Americans who had been taken hostage in Tehran. From the expression on his father's face, the old man wasn't convinced. "What about your own experiences?"

"You know I don't talk about that."

"Yes, I know, but you can at least tell me why you left. I don't want to hear one more time how you just wanted to do something new."

Janusz considered the request. He figured it was time to tell him the truth—at least a part of it. "Well, dad, if you must know, I left because in the end I was no longer willing to compromise my values."

"What does that mean?"

"It means the bosses wanted to terminate an operation I felt was needed to continue, so I disagreed."

"What happened then?"

"I made my disapproval known."

"How?"

"Well, how should I put this? Yes. I told my managers that they could go 'fuck themselves' in those exact words."

"Jesus!"

"Obviously, they didn't agree with my observations, which prompted them to file charges. However, when I threatened to complain to Congress, the situation resolved itself. At that point, I figured instead of staying at a place where my opinions were not valued, it would be better to find employment elsewhere."

"I'm sure there is more to this story, but I'm proud of you for standing up for your beliefs."

"Thanks! That's how I see it too."

What he didn't tell his father was that he had not been alone. There were other patriots determined to maintain America's security despite the imposed restrictions. Janusz considered himself lucky to have discovered who these people were and what they were doing.

The elder Soltani suddenly glanced over at his son with a concerned expression on his face. "Janusz, are you sure that's all there is to that story? Was there any other reason you may have left?"

Janusz wanted to change the subject but thought it would be best to tackle this head-on. "What do you mean? What other reason could there be?"

"Nothing. Nothing at all, but parents always worry. By the way, are you still going to therapy?" his father inquired diplomatically.

"Yes, of course!"

"So, I take it, everything is now under control? You haven't been calling Las Vegas late into the evening?"

"No, I haven't been gambling if that's what you're getting at. As I told you and Mom before, I've been seeing someone who's helping me deal with this. Please don't concern yourself with the issue any longer. It's done with. You've got enough to worry about at the hospital."

"You're right, Janusz. I do have enough to worry about at the hospital. I'm glad you're taking the bull by the horns on this one. I only want the best for you, son."

"I know, Dad. I know." Janusz stood up to hug his father and say goodbye to his mother. It was imperative to get to Arlington to rest up for the next day.

After a seemingly endless drive, during which he almost dozed off behind the wheel, Janusz arrived at his townhouse. It had been paid for mostly from his early gambling wins. These days, it appeared every one of his bets turned into a loss. Things had deteriorated to the point that Janusz was worried his betting activities were beginning to affect his relationship with Jennifer, whom he met years earlier at The Farm, the CIA's training center for field operatives. They were part of the same incoming class.

She was asleep now, but there were many things he would have to answer for when she awakened in the morning. He badly needed his rest. Perhaps that was the reason he'd been feeling like shit, both physically and mentally.

4. MALARD MISSILE RESEARCH FACILITY, WESTERN TEHRAN, IRAN

October 12

Today was going to be his day. Standing inside the observation room, the director, a major general in the IRGC Aerospace Forces, sweated profusely as he watched his men inside the fuel lab. They were mixing an experimental propellant developed for Iran's newest missile. He was pacing like an expectant father in the waiting room of the hospital. He had planted the seed for this program over two decades ago. Since then, he'd been personally responsible for every success as Iran's embryonic missile program achieved its various milestones. Now, close to thirty years later, he was waiting for that magical moment when his colleagues would utter the precious word every expectant father wanted to hear— "Congratulations!" The batch was the latest version of hydroxy-terminated polybutadiene (HTPB), a type of solid propellant missile fuel. His team was preparing the fuel for a static motor test.

The phone rang in the observation room of the IRGC Malard research facility. He was engrossed in watching the activity in the fuel lab behind the blast-proof windows. His blood boiled as soon as he recognized the voice. An agitated President Azari of the Islamic Republic of Iran was on the other end of the line. The president got right down to business.

"How are you coming along on the fuel mix? More importantly, when can we commence the final phase of the project?"

"As I've explained to you before, the work with missile fuels is a slightly more delicate operation than making kabobs. My men have to observe very strict safety precautions. The slightest mistake can lead to a catastrophic explosion. Having said that, we should have the appropriate fuel ready within the next few weeks. I can't give you an exact date yet." The two men had known each other for years, which allowed the director to speak frankly and somewhat sarcastically to the president.

"Very well, our group is ready to move as soon as you've completed your end. Let me remind you once again that time is not on our side. Ayatollah Mashhadi is as suspicious as ever about those conspiring against the regime. His spies in the IRGC intelligence organization (IRGC-IO) and his representatives throughout the government are breathing down my neck every day. All will be lost if we wait much longer."

"Have faith, Hamid. Any effort to bring back Imam Mahdi is full of dangers and setbacks. We've waited a thousand years for this moment, so we can wait a bit longer. I'll call you again in —"

Before he could finish his sentence, there was a flash of light, and the entire facility shook violently. For a second, he had a flashback to his days as the commander of an artillery unit during the Iran-Iraq War. He hung up with the president still on the line. The lights suddenly went out. A second later, the building was lit with the strange red glow of the emergency lighting system. The director peered through the glass of the blast-proof door. Inside the fuel lab, thick smoke filled the air. Without warning, the sprinkler system activated, helping to douse the fire. As the smoke settled, four of his men, with whom he'd spoken just twenty minutes earlier, were burned beyond recognition. The only good news was that the stench of their burning flesh could not reach him behind the air-tight door.

By the time the fire rescue team entered the lab, it was too late. There remained only four heaps of burning flesh on the floor surrounding the mixer. What was once human skin had turned completely black with red blotches of blood oozing out. The intense heat from the explosion caused the men's intestines to burst out of their abdominal cavities onto the floor. The smoke emanating from the still-burning corpses gave the appearance of a macabre barbecue. He walked around the room taking deep breaths to calm his nerves. His team was cutting too many corners to speed up the program, and now they were paying the price with human lives. He cared deeply for each of the men working for him, but he was determined not to let the grief overwhelm him. There was too much at stake now.

That evening, the director was back in his office rehearsing the lines of condolence he would convey to the dead men's relatives. The sound of someone calling his name came out of nowhere.

"Afshin, why the hell didn't you knock before you walked in on me? Can't you see I've got a lot on my mind?" Originally from Shiraz, Afshin was an engineer in the propulsion team, whose star was on the rise. He appeared older than his thirty-five years due to his receding hairline and a week's worth of facial hair, the signature look of the IRGC. Unlike many Iranians, he had not undergone rhinoplasty to shrink his bulbous nose. He was one of the cockiest men under the director's command, but he was a superb engineer.

"I did call your name, Ostad, but no one answered. When I walked in, you were in a catatonic state, so I spoke louder." *Ostad*, the Persian word for professor, was the term Afshin and his colleagues used as a sign of respect toward their mentor.

"I'm getting ready to call the next of kin of our colleagues. After that, I need to go home to my family. Whatever you want to tell me, better make it quick."

"Ostad, we're having problems with the industrial mixers that the head office has acquired for us. When started, the mixers spin at a normal rate, but after a few minutes on any given setting, they spin much faster than they're supposed to. Given the volatility of the chemicals involved, this can result in a catastrophic explosion similar to the one earlier today. The head of security wants us to wait two weeks before we mix new batches of experimental fuels while he scrutinizes the procurement network trail for signs of sabotage."

"May Allah curse those damn Americans! This has to be their handiwork. We spent three times the market price to procure top-of-the-line industrial mixers from our clandestine network, yet we still have to deal with this bullshit." The Director sighed. "Not to worry, the Americans will soon get their reward. In the meantime, I'd anticipated something like this. We've established our own assembly lines for both the three-thousand-liter and the fifty-one-hundred-liter mixers at our factory in Parchin. I'll get you two brand new mixers in less than half that time. Now, if you cannot think of any reason to further delay this program, I'll go home to rest."

"Very well, Ostad. With your guidance and Allah's blessing, I'm certain we'll acquire the needed fuel ahead of schedule." As Afshin walked away, the director checked one last thing before going home. He was expecting an email from Mr. Xian Li, a retired colonel in the People's Liberation Army of China (PLA). On the side, Mr. Li was an enterprising capitalist like most of his compatriots. He had established an underground company that provided hard-to-come-by equipment for sanctioned regimes. Among the services provided were schematics for building centrifuges that spun uranium hexafluoride (UF6) gas to separate the heavier U235 isotopes from the more prevalent U238. The leftover batch of "enriched uranium" could be used to make either fuel rods or the core of a nuclear weapon. Mr. Li was particular about the information he was willing to provide to clients for fear that the technology provided was too sensitive. He risked execution by the Chinese authorities.

The director was communicating directly with Mr. Li, presenting himself as a procurement agent for Gulf Limited LLC. He had asked Mr. Li to sell the fuel formula the PLA used for its solid-fueled long-range missiles. The director offered to pay Mr. Li five million dollars for his services, but Mr. Li was hesitant. This was one of those sensitive technologies that carried the death penalty if provided to adversaries.

The director walked down the hallway to an office administered by the IRGC Cyber Defense Command. The prolonged standing was painful for his feet. His back tormented him with each step. His eyelids were so heavy that it was a struggle to keep them open. The three computers in this room were each a stand-alone—they were neither connected to an internal network nor to each other. Their hard drives had been wiped clean. There was also no capacity to store data on these machines. They were used only to surf the web and to send query emails on behalf of the missile program. The director checked the email address under the fake name Jamshid.irani@smail.com. There was one email from bruce.a.smith21@smail.com, Mr. Li's online persona. He clicked on the unopened envelope, and out popped the following message:

> *Dear Mr. Irani,*
> *Thank you for your inquiry to become a supplier of our soap in your country. Unfortunately, our board of directors has decided that we are presently not ready to expand operations into your country. We, therefore, regret that we will not be able to furnish you with the formula to manufacture our soap. However, please feel free to reach out to us in the future as we may be able to explore other business opportunities with you.*
> *Sincerely,*
> *Bruce Smith.*

The coded language was Mr. Li's way of rejecting the director's request.

"May Allah curse that wretched Yazid! These damn chinky-eyed Chinese are impossible." The name "Yazid" was always taken in vain by Shi'a Iranians when they became upset. Yazid was a seventh-century Sunni caliph who killed the third Shi'a Prophet, Imam Hussein, in the battle of Karbala. The director was not only exhausted, but he was also fuming about the latest setback to the program. He had no choice but to utilize the clandestine missile procurement network that Iran had established in the 1990s to circumvent western sanctions.

After deleting the email, he used the icon of the IRGC Cyber Defense Command to wipe the computer's memory. His mind was racing. Ayatollah Mashhadi's spies were certain to discover his plans one of these days. He was so tired he could barely think, but there was a lot of work to be done. He had another trick up his sleeve to help the program stay on track. The director decided it was best to spend the night on the floor of his office in a sleeping bag. Yet another night away from his family, but no sacrifice was too great for the return of Imam Mahdi.

5. OFFICE OF THE IRANIAN PRESIDENT, CENTRAL TEHRAN, IRAN

October 13

President Hamid Azari-Tabar stormed out of his office inside the Presidential Palace in the Pasteur District of Tehran. He moved with the determination of a man on a mission. He wore his usual tan slacks, an open-collared dress shirt, and a tan sports jacket. His beard was neatly trimmed. He had scheduled a morning meeting with a group of advisors, but these men were not at the Presidential Palace as part of their official duties. President Azari stood one hundred fifty-eight centimeters on a good day. He carried a huge chip on his shoulders, wanting to prove that he was every bit as competent and ruthless as the taller men around him. Despite the fact that the president was officially the second most powerful man in Iran, after the Supreme Leader himself, he was determined to use the opportunity given to him by the Iranian electorate to make his mark on the national scene. President Azari, who was not a cleric, had come to the conclusion that his term in office would be used to set the stage for the return of the Hidden Imam Mahdi.

His upbringing in the poor neighborhoods of South Tehran made it easier for the average Iranian to identify with him, thereby helping him win the election. President Azari's family was devoutly Shi'a. Their brand of Shi'ism could hardly be described as mainstream, however. They were, in fact, devoted to the cult of the Twelfth Shi'a Imam, the Mahdi. The president had grown up believing that Imam Mahdi's return was near. Therefore, no effort should be spared to hasten this event. As he moved up the political ladder, he had aligned himself with groups who were also devoted followers of Imam Mahdi, endeavoring to assist his return. These men now comprised the majority of his cabinet and senior advisors. He had helped more than a few of them rise to the highest levels of the Iranian military.

President Azari convened the meeting promptly at eight in the morning with his customary *"Bismillah Rahman Rahim,"* *In the name of God, the Merciful.* The other five men gathered around the table included Admiral Ali-Reza Abbasi, the Defense Minister, and Mohsen Jafarzadeh, the commander of the IRGC. Also seated at the table was Ayatollah Yadollah Boroujerdi, the Supreme Leader's representative, who ensured political ideological conformity in the Armed Forces. That meant he was also head of the Political Ideological Directorate (PID) in the Armed Forces General Staff. The PID served a similar function to the Zampolit, the political officers in the former Soviet Union whose job was to ensure that all military officials were loyal to both the Communist Party and its top leaders. Sitting to the right of Jafarzadeh was Mojtaba Vatanparast, the head of the IRGC Aerospace Forces, the organization in charge of all IRGC air force and missile units. Finally, there was Akbar Javadpoor, the IRGC Missile Forces Commander who was sitting to the left of Jafarzadeh.

These were some of the highest-ranking military officials in the Islamic Republic of Iran, who also happened to be members of the secret Hojjatieh society. President Azari glanced around the table with a smile. If he didn't present the news properly, his audience might panic. He inhaled before speaking.

"Gentlemen, we have a big problem. There's been a delay with the development of the fuel. We cannot move forward before our esteemed colleague, the director at Malard, has a reliable propellant for the Buraq missile. During our last conversation, he briefed me about an explosion in his lab that killed four technicians. I'm sorry to inform you that I still don't have an exact date to operationalize our plan."

His audience was incredulous. The distinguished collection of plotters spoke out all at once until it was impossible to hear anything other than a loud buzz. President Azari slammed his fist on the table, "Gentlemen, we're not in the bazaar. Please speak up one at a time."

"How can this be, Mr. President?" Defense Minister Abbasi was the first to speak. "When you first approached us a year ago about the idea for hastening the return of Imam Mahdi, you said the director had already overcome all the technical difficulties for the Buraq project. Now you're telling us there is a delay in the work related to the propellant. This entire plan depends on the director's ability to deliver the missiles in a timely manner."

General Javadpoor quickly jumped in. "I'm also disturbed by this setback. My men have not yet rehearsed this plan. I cannot recruit for this operation until we're certain that a proven fuel is ready for delivery. The longer we sit on this, the greater the chance that Ayatollah Mashhadi's spies will shut us down."

President Azari's frustration with the group came to a boil. His face contorted into a scowl. He was overcome by the thought that his audience didn't have confidence in his abilities. He had helped all of them rise through the ranks. There was nothing he hated more than ingrates.

"Gentlemen, I'm well aware of the risks this group is taking. You must all remember that we're setting the stage for the return of Imam Mahdi. If that were an easy task, previous generations would have beaten us to it by now. Anyone of you not worthy of the challenge can walk away at any time."

President Azari's comments had the intended impact. The group was now silent.

"Obviously, we've experienced a setback. That doesn't matter because we're fighting on the side of justice. When the *Seyed-ol-Shohada*, Imam Hussein himself, went out against the forces of Yazid, he was aware he might not succeed. If millions of people have to die to make this happen, then so be it!" The president regained his composure.

"I've authorized the Buraq Project director to utilize a portion of the national budget ordinarily allocated for the construction of highways. We'll use the money for a clandestine operation to procure fuel from foreign experts. The Director assures me that his contacts in the Far East have what we need. In the meantime, you'll carry on as usual in your day jobs until further notice. This meeting is adjourned."

As the group walked out, President Azari worried that one of his comrades would reveal their intentions to the IRGC-IO. Perhaps he needed more informants to keep track of his closest advisors. One thing was clear. Without progress on the fuel, the plans for the return of Imam Mahdi would not see the light of day.

6. MALARD MISSILE RESEARCH FACILITY, WESTERN TEHRAN, IRAN

October 14

The director arrived at the Malard missile research facility exactly at seven-thirty in the morning. He drove to his usual parking spot in front of the main research hangar, located off a two-lane highway near the Tehran suburb of Karaj. Malard was built according to the director's wishes, which included painting all surfaces in blue, the color of his favorite team in the Iranian Professional Football League.

It took the director a little over a minute to walk from his car to the main research hangar where prototypes of a variety of missile motors and nozzles were in various stages of development. He was particularly excited about a new batch of 3-meter-diameter missile motors. This was the first set of carbon composite motors that the IRGC missile team had produced. Standard missile motors were usually made of metals such as aluminum or titanium. The problem faced by rocket engineers was that these metals were relatively heavy, and they required a powerful fuel to propel them to great distances. With the use of composite motors, the IRGC would have the opportunity to launch its missiles to greater distances using fuels with lower specific impulses (SI). SI was the measure used to indicate the efficiency of the rocket propellant. A higher SI number meant that less propellant was needed to impart a given momentum to the rocket. To date, the director's team had only been able to make solid rocket fuels with SIs in the low two hundreds.

In order to lob its missiles to the required distances, the IRGC needed to do two things— decrease the weight of the missile components, such as the motor or nozzle frames, and produce a rocket fuel with SIs closer to the three hundred range. Since the program had been having difficulty increasing the SI of its fuels, the director had been pushing the composites team to start manufacturing missile components using carbon fibers.

He was here to conduct an inspection of the teams in the program and to get an update on their progress. The director was recognized as the father of Iran's missile program. He was head of the very first team sent to Syria in 1984 for training on the Scud missiles Iran had purchased from North Korea.

The director arrived in front of a carbon composite motor that had been rolled out the previous evening when someone called his name.

"Ostad, I spoke with the Aerospace Industries Organization. The mixers are ready. They need a date for delivery." Afshin said.

The director grew furious. "*Ya Abolfazl,*" he shouted in disbelief. "Tell them we've been ready to receive our mixers all along. They should know our program has top priority. From now on, I expect them to deliver our equipment as soon as they have it in hand."

The head of the missile program shuffled around the floor while inspecting the various stations with his entourage. He was surrounded by several IRGC guards from the Ansar al-Mahdi division, responsible for the protection of government VIPs. Also in attendance was Massoud Hosseinzadeh who had joined the IRGC after his high school graduation. Massoud had graduated at the top of his class from the Alborz Technical High School in Tehran, the best math/science high school in the entire country. The year that he took the *concour*, the Iranian comprehensive college entrance exam, he had ranked second in the entire country out of a pool of six hundred fifty thousand students.

The director gazed at a man atop a high plank working

on a section of a carbon-composite motor frame. The man was completely engrossed in his work.

"Massoud, who is that man?" the director said, pointing toward the high plank.

"That's Fariborz Shadnamah, Ostad. He's one of our best technicians when it comes to carbon-composite materials."

The director walked underneath the plank while waving his hand to say hello.

Fariborz looked down. A man was waving below him. He muttered to himself, "Who the fuck is the annoying bastard trying to break my concentration?" He politely waved back before resuming his work.

The man below was persistent. "Hello, up there! May Allah grant you eternal strength!"

Fariborz wanted to scream at the stranger who had now extended his hand to shake his. Considering the possibility that the stranger might be a VIP, Fariborz climbed down. They stood face-to-face as the man that Fariborz didn't recognize patted him on the back.

"May Imam Mahdi choose you to be among the leaders of his army!" the man said before walking away.

Fariborz stood baffled. Why had this man taken him away from his work to praise him with a string of unsolicited blessings? His comrades approached, laughing.

"Guys, what kind of a joke is this? Who the hell is that guy, and why is he here?" Fariborz said.

A colleague replied, "You still don't know who that was, dumbass? Perhaps you were an Arab in a previous life. That's the director of this program."

Fariborz blushed with embarrassment. He was grateful that he hadn't insulted the man for disturbing his work.

After another thirty minutes of walking around to meet with the various teams, the director stepped out of the main research hangar to walk back to his office. Massoud accompanied him now. A serious student, he had studied chemical engineering at the prestigious Sharif University of Technology and had earned a BS and a PhD at the IRGC's Imam Hussein University (IHU) in aerospace engineering. He chose the program because IHU had one of the only two large wind tunnels in Iran for conducting research on airplanes and missiles. He knew that he would one day lead the IRGC's burgeoning missile program.

"Ostad, we're making tremendous strides. I expect completion of research on the fuel once we get our new mixer installed."

"That's actually what I want to talk to you about, Massoud. We don't have a lot of time. We have to take a shortcut to procure our solid fuel from abroad," the director said, placing a hand on his shoulder. "I'm glad we're outside as this wasn't an easy decision for me. I've decided to make Afshin the head of the propulsion team."

The former commander of the propulsion program had recently died in a car crash on his way home from a vacation near the Caspian Sea. This had not been shocking news, given the high fatality rate on Iran's highways. Perhaps things would be better if the government provided more funds for infrastructure projects.

Massoud had always been under the impression that he and the director had a special bond that could not be put into words. It was the type of bond that, in Massoud's mind, developed between a father and son. The protégé had visions of following in the mentor's footsteps as head of Iran's missile program.

"I know you've been after that appointment. However, Afshin has more management experience than you. Under present time constraints, I believe placing him as head of the propulsion team will lead to quicker results. There is something else that I've got in mind for you."

41

Massoud was suddenly in deep thought.

"Massoud, are you listening to me?"

"Sorry, Ostad. I'm a bit tired. What did you say?"

"I said I've booked round-trip tickets for you and a team under your supervision to Kuala Lumpur. You're to make contact with several suppliers I've lined up in Malaysia. You leave tomorrow. Any questions?"

"No, sir. Your instructions are crystal clear."

"May Allah grant you eternal health and success!"

Massoud was plotting his next move as his mentor said goodbye.

7. GULF LIMITED LLC, DUBAI, UAE

14 October

Farzad Gilani's father had paid close to twenty thousand dollars to buy an exemption for his military service. Farzad was from a prominent merchant family in Tehran with connections to many of the world's trade hubs. On the surface, he had no visible connections to the Iranian government, a situation that both he and the Islamic Republic went out of their way to maintain. One of his specialties was establishing companies in countries with no ties to Iran. These front companies were then free to buy or sell any commodity that was forbidden to companies registered in Iran or owned by Iranians. Farzad requested the citizens of countries such as Luxemburg, UAE, Malaysia, or Singapore to establish corporations with the sole purpose of procuring sanctioned items for the Iranian regime in exchange for money. The items bought could then be shipped to several locations before arriving in Iran.

Iranian money was stashed in banks located around the world. The money eventually arrived in the account of an individual, like Farzad Gilani, who could purchase items needed by the Iranian government. These funds could also be transferred to Iranian proxies abroad without ever being touched by an Iranian citizen or financial institution. The Iranians were the best in the world at circumventing sanctions. As a matter of fact, there was a whole generation of rich Iranian entrepreneurs whose specialty was to act as intermediaries for the regime in Tehran in return for a percentage of the transaction costs. Several Iranian billionaires had started out this way. Farzad Gilani was hoping to join their ranks. He had come to the UAE two weeks earlier to incorporate a company in Dubai for the IRGC. Several Emiratis received a handsome sum to establish Gulf Limited LLC. The management of Gulf Limited subsequently hired a sales representative to travel to Malaysia on a special assignment.

8. JANUSZ'S TOWNHOUSE, ARLINGTON, VA

October 16

Janusz and Jennifer were getting ready for dinner at their favorite Persian restaurant, The Kabob House. He had two tickets to a ballet at the Kennedy Center for later in the evening. He often wondered why he had fallen for her in the first place. Perhaps it was her auburn hair and blue eyes, a perfect combination for her delightful face. Her statuesque body and toned buttocks never failed to set his libido on fire. More importantly, she had been supportive of his decision to leave the CIA when he told her about the issues he was experiencing.

Jennifer was from Minnesota, where her entire family still lived. She was the first in her family to move out of the land of ten thousand lakes. After graduating Phi Beta Kappa from the University of Minnesota, she enrolled in the Master's program at Johns Hopkins University (School of Advanced International Studies) in Washington, D.C. Her connection with a recruiter had ultimately led to a job offer from the CIA, which she excitedly accepted. Her concentration in international relations and her fluency in Arabic had paid off. She started dating Janusz during their first year at The Farm, the CIA's training camp. Romances between trainees were so common that those who trained there referred to it as the world's most expensive dating agency.

"It was nice of you to finally make time for me with your busy schedule. Fighting terrorists and betting on sports leaves little time for much else, doncha know?" Jennifer said.

"I love it when the Minnesota in you comes out. I'm sorry I haven't been able to spend more time with you. I'll make it up to you, I promise."

"Eh! Truth be told, I don't mind it much when you blow me off for work. What I do mind is all the time you spend studying sports statistics so you can place your bets. That's getting old!"

"Speaking of which, did you watch the hockey game last night? The Minnesota Wild beat the Capitals by three goals." Janusz mentioned her favorite franchise in the hope of distracting her.

"Don't change the subject," she said with a hand on her hip and a familiar eye roll. "In all seriousness, you need to start making decisions. I mean, what do you care more about—me or betting on sports?"

Janusz's shoulders slumped slightly, but she continued.

"I'm not saying you have to stop watching sports. But how you bet is self-destructive, and it worries me. I don't want to watch you do this to yourself, I can't. And I won't."

For no particular reason, he suddenly remembered that horrible Christmas Eve when he had rear-ended an SUV on the way back from a party in D.C. He had been drinking and shouldn't have gotten behind the wheel. Rather than risk his arrest for a DUI and the loss of his security clearance, Jennifer quickly asked him to change seats with her. She hadn't drunk that night, but she took a hit on her auto insurance. When the police arrived, all they did was write a report of the incident instead of arresting Janusz for drunk driving. When he thought about it, she had been better to him than any woman, except his own mother. She had even given him the money to pay off his gambling debts, not too long ago, to the tune of thirty-five hundred dollars. Janusz had paid her back, of course, but that was beside the point. She had never asked "why" when he approached her for the money.

"Are you trying to tell me I've become a gambler?"

"No! That's not what I'm saying." She paused. "Well, maybe that's what I'm saying."

"I told you, that's all behind me now. I've been working on it."

"Are you sure?"

"Of course, I'm sure. What do you mean?"

"Well," She bit her bottom lip as though she didn't want the words to come out of her mouth. Then, with a sigh, she said, "Just last week, I wanted to surprise you with something naughty. I was going to slip a pair of my panties into your desk for you to find when you least expected it. Instead, you surprised me. Do you know what I found?" Her cheeks began turning pink as she tried to control the volume of her voice. Janusz stared at her in silence.

"Five thousand dollars in cash—that's what! Tell me, who has that kind of money lying around in their desk? And why?"

"I didn't think I have to explain everything I do in this house, but since you're so interested, those five thousand dollars were for the presents I buy for the kids at the hospital," Janusz said.

"Uff-da, do you really expect me to believe that?" Janusz gave no reply. It was futile to try to defend himself. He opted for another tactic.

"Oh shit!" Janusz patted the front and back pockets of his pants before working his way up to his shirt. "Do you have the tickets for the show?"

"No, we're picking them up at will call, remember? I know you said it's a surprise, but will you tell me what show we're going to watch tonight?"

Janusz savored the moment. "Well, I hate to give it away, but I got us two front row seats for Tchaikovsky's *Swan Lake*." It was her favorite ballet.

"Are you pulling my leg, Janusz? If you are, you're officially a dead man, doncha know?" The peppering of her sentence with Minnesota speak was a good sign.

"I'd never joke about a thing like that. Now hurry up and

get dressed so we can get to dinner. I'm starving."

"I know exactly whatcha mean. I could eat a whole deer myself right about now," Jennifer said.

As he walked to the foyer to grab the coats, his cell phone rang. He answered hesitantly when he glanced at the caller ID.

"Hey Tony, nice of you to think of me after work. I'm catching a show at the Kennedy Center, and I'm late for dinner."

"Sorry to rain on your parade. Cancel all your plans, and come back to headquarters at once."

"You gotta be shitting me!"

"Afraid not, we have a bit of a situation on our hands."
Janusz moaned loudly before giving his reply. "I'll be there within the hour." He didn't know how he was going to explain canceling *Swan Lake* to Jennifer. Things were about to get ugly even before he made it to the office.

9. UNIT 81 HEADQUARTERS, HERNDON, VA

October 16

Thedrive to Herndon took less than half the usual time. He went straight up to the sixth-floor conference room where Tony and the others were already seated. They all stared as he walked through the door.

"What's up? Do I have a cock coming out of my forehead?" Janusz's attempt at humor fell on deaf ears.

Tony broke the silence. "We had an interesting meeting earlier today with Jason from the SSCI. Apparently, the Iranian IRGC has been working on a clandestine missile project that we aren't aware of."

Jason Osborne, the chief of staff at the SSCI, was an expert intelligence analyst. The SSCI received briefings from the Intelligence Community on the most pressing threats facing the country as a part of its oversight duties. Jason worked for the Committee Chair, Senator Donald Patrick. The initial agreement creating the Unit in 1981 included a provision that the SSCI would review the most difficult intelligence challenges when there was no consensus for action. They would then pass the problem over to the folks in the Unit for an independent review. The SSCI would provide the Unit with all the relevant intelligence that the IC had gathered on the topic. This would allow the Unit to decide whether it wanted to investigate the matter any further for evidence of threats to US national security. If an imminent threat was identified, the Unit would use the resources at its disposal to tackle the problem with an "all-gloves-off" approach.

Janusz's demeanor changed completely. The topic of Iran always garnered his complete attention. "What did our friends on the Hill have to say about this?"

Stan picked up where Tony left off. "Less than 24 hours ago, a walk-in made contact with the CIA in Kuala Lumpur. He claimed access to sources in the IRGC. He then told the Agency officer that the IRGC is now developing its own missiles, and he would be willing to provide more detailed information about the project if the CIA agreed to deposit two million dollars into a bank account he maintained in Malaysia. He also requested asylum in the United States for himself and his family."

"What did the Agency tell him?"

"What do you think they told him? They thought he was a quack who was trying to hustle them for money. They thanked him for his time and shooed him away."

"Why?"

"The CIA believes he is lying because the Aerospace Industries Organization runs the missile program in Iran. The Agency insists that the IRGC only controls the missiles once they're built by the Aerospace Industries Organization."

"So, who is this guy?"

"We don't know yet. The Agency has never heard of him either."

"Are you telling me they won't meet with him again?"

"Afraid not. They didn't even bother to brief this to the NSC. Jason only came across the information by chance. Lucky for us, he reads through all the operational traffic that no one else has the patience for."

As a part of the oversight agreement to keep the SSCI informed of all its activities, the CIA had agreed to provide access at one of its secure office facilities in Northern Virginia to SSCI staffers. The SSCI staffers drove out to a building conveniently located in a business park near the Unit's headquarters in Herndon. They subsequently took the elevators down to a basement vault set up especially for them. They were provided with badges and individual passwords that identified unique users each time they visited the facility. Behind the metal vault door was a room with twelve computers connected to the classified CIA network where the staffers had access to field cables, CIA assessments, and personality profiles. They also had access to a customized search engine that allowed them to pull information on any given intelligence topic produced by the sixteen other agencies in the US IC. The only restriction was that they were not allowed to print or take any files out of the facility without first informing their CIA liaison.

Tony jumped in. "Janusz, the SSCI suggested we investigate the matter. After talking it over, this afternoon, we've decided to authorize the necessary funding for you to tackle this as your next project. Take as many people from here or from the folks in Melbourne. We don't know how long the IRGC has been able to keep this program a secret." Tony turned to face the rest of the group. "Time is not on our side here, people."

The minute the words "Iran" and "missiles" were mentioned in the same sentence, Janusz was convinced that this was a worthy mission. The timing could not be worse. Jennifer wouldn't wait much longer. This project could delay his plans for weeks, if not months.

10. THE OCEANA COMPANY, MELBOURNE, AUSTRALIA

October 18

The Emirates Air flight from Dubai arrived on time. Half an hour later, Janusz breezed through customs using his Australian passport. He walked out of the terminal to catch a cab to Oceana's office building on 101 Collins Street downtown. The one he entered had leather seats, TV monitors, and wood side panels. It was a cab for VIPs.

"Where to?"

"101 Collins Street."

The cab driver treated Janusz as a captive audience. He couldn't stop talking about his family from Lebanon and their journey to Australia. Janusz's face reminded the driver of a friend in a Christian neighborhood of Beirut. This prompted the driver to inquire if Janusz was originally from the Middle East. Janusz tersely answered that he was Polish, but he wouldn't rule anything out. The driver chuckled as he pushed through the morning traffic on the M2 expressway. Janusz stared out the window, reflecting on Tony's wisdom in setting up an Australian private equity firm named The Oceana Company. One advantage of the Australian firm was the ability to fly below the radar in most parts of the world. Very few questioned the activities of an Australian company to the same extent as an American one.

The more important advantage was a quirk in Australian law, allowing its citizens to change their legal name once every twelve months. They could then apply for a new passport with each name change. After learning about these loopholes in Australian law, Tony had transferred a select group to Australia as employees of Oceana.

Australia was a secret organization's wet dream. Janusz was eager to return to the condominium on 101 Collins Street. He also had a great sense of urgency to get started. Why hadn't the CIA followed up with the walk-in in Kuala Lumpur? After years of Political Correctness, this fabled agency had turned into a debating society. The Unit, however, didn't have the luxury to let this matter slide.

Oceana owned floors thirty to thirty-three in one of the fanciest buildings in Melbourne. Several of the world's most prestigious private equity firms, including Lazard, had offices in 101 Collins Street. The location provided a strong backstop for Oceana's employees. Two of those floors had been purchased as condominiums for personnel stationed in Australia. The other two floors housed offices and conference rooms. Janusz was assigned to one of the condos on the thirty-third floor. It enabled him to play the part of a successful private equity hotshot. The Unit's front company, HRC, had spared no expense to create that image for the team members in Australia. It was one of the perks of the job. His only regret was that his family and friends were not around when he was in town on business.

Once he was settled, he spent the rest of the afternoon researching articles about the IRGC's missile program. He supplemented this material by going through all the files provided by the Unit on the topic. There were a few pages of notes about the meeting with the walk-in at the embassy in Kuala Lumpur. These reports had been specifically rewritten to mimic a movie script with real names replaced by pseudonyms.

Since the Unit didn't operate out of embassies or have access to secure government facilities, it found other methods of safeguarding the classified information entrusted to its employees by the Senate Intelligence Committee. The Unit removed the names of real people and places and wrote the events as if it were a screenplay. It was enough for the field operative to get a brief background on the target. After reading the cable about the Kuala Lumpur source, Janusz fell into a deep sleep. He woke up the next morning at seven-thirty to the sound of his alarm. There was just enough time to take a shower and shave before meeting with the rest of the team in the conference room two floors below.

After taking a sip of water, Janusz gave the team a summary of what he had learned in Herndon. Everything about this case indicated the Unit needed to make contact with the source to get to the bottom of his story. Something was missing in the chain of events. He feared that the missing information would eventually cost American lives. They decided the best way forward was to track down the source. The only lead they had was a cellular telephone number written down by the CIA officer who had interviewed him.

11.THE GRAND HYATT HOTEL, KUALA LUMPUR, MALAYSIA

October 20

The phone rang in room 3014 of the Grand Hyatt in Kuala Lumpur.

"Hello, sir, I'm calling from the US Embassy regarding your recent visit."

"Who's this?"

"Name is Derrick. It's regarding the request you made to Frank the other day at the embassy." Frank Berkoff was the pseudonym of the CIA officer to whom the source had spoken when he visited the embassy four days earlier.

"Yes. I thought your people weren't interested in what I had to offer."

"There's been a change in our management recently. The new manager would like us to sit down with you again. Can you meet at the Malay Palace restaurant tonight at seven-thirty?"

Eric Bradford, an employee of the Unit using the cover name Derrick, tried to be as discreet as possible. Janusz was listening close by.

"Yes, I know where that is. Whom should I ask for?"

"Just grab a table and wear a dark suit with a white pocket square on the outside. I'll find you!"

As soon as he hung up, Eric got the thumbs-up sign from Janusz along with a lecture on safety. "When you see this guy, tell him we may be willing to pay him the two million dollars that he requested on one condition—he gives us a summary of what he knows. We'll determine if the information is worth the price. If he agrees to our terms, tell him you'll reach out with further instructions."

"Got it."

"Remember, we're nearby. Pull the knob on your watch if you need us. Good luck!"

Eric was known for his sense of humor. Whether a friend needed a ride from the airport at midnight or a loan for a few thousand dollars, he never let anyone down. He was loyal—to his country, his friends, and especially to Janusz. Like most of his colleagues, Eric had worked in the CIA as an operations officer before joining HRC. Similar to Janusz, he was turned off by the bureaucratic culture of that organization, both risk-averse and opposed to initiative. The last straw was being passed over for a promotion because a colleague deceitfully reported him for verbal abuse. Although not true, the incident had allowed his rival to get the promotion. The Unit had hired Eric only a year before Janusz. It was he who had brought Janusz to the attention of the senior leadership at the Unit. The better pay and greater opportunity at HRC had allowed Eric to afford a more comfortable lifestyle for his wife and two children, a son and daughter, all of whom were in Australia. He was excellent at his job and a dapper dresser, clean cut with short blond hair and blue eyes.

Eric wore striped navy slacks with a white dress shirt open at the collar. His black loafers were handmade in Italy. When he arrived at the Malay Palace, at seven-twenty in the evening, the source was already seated at a corner at the far end of the room. The entire restaurant was dimly lit with candles at the center of all the tables. Eric approached the source casually. He observed the scruff-faced Iranian wearing a dark suit, a white shirt with no tie, and a white pocket square.

"Hello, I'm Derrick. May I sit down?"

The source's face didn't betray his emotions. He motioned with his hand for the American to sit across from him without introducing himself.

"I hope you won't be offended if I tell you that my colleagues didn't provide me with your name."

"No problem. You may call me Nasser."

"I'm very pleased you accepted our invitation to meet again, Nasser. We'd like to continue the conversation you had with Frank at the embassy. Would you be willing to talk to one of our people tomorrow so we may get an overview of your story? We'll arrange a more thorough meeting at a later date in a house we have outside of Kuala Lumpur."

"You tell me the time and place for tomorrow's meeting, and I'll be there," Nasser said.

"We can send one of our men to your hotel for the initial meeting if you prefer. How does seven in the evening sound?"

Nasser appeared to weigh the implications of meeting with a CIA man in his own hotel. He quietly offered his American guest a menu already on the table.

"Tomorrow at seven in the Grand Hyatt will be fine on one condition. I expect a down payment of ten percent on the two million."

"I believe that can be arranged."

"Very well. Shall we order something from the menu so our rendezvous here does not appear out of place?"

"I couldn't agree more, Nasser. I've eaten here before. I highly recommend any of their chicken dishes, which are all superb."

After an hour of small talk during dinner, Nasser and Eric shook hands outside the Malay Palace. They then set off in opposite directions.

12. ON THE WAY TO A
MEETING, KUALA LUMPUR, MALAYSIA

October 21

J anusz's brain was on autopilot as he made his way through the streets of Kuala Lumpur for the meeting. The thought crossed his mind that it was rather ironic that the Iranian revolution of 1979 had started out as a struggle for freedom against the excesses of Shah Mohammad Reza Pahlavi. The end result, however, was the religious despotism of Shi'a clerics that turned out to be even more stifling. The forced conversion of majority Sunni Iranians to Shi'a Islam occurred during the sixteenth century under pressure from the Safavid Dynasty. Initially, the clerical class was content with advising the king behind the scenes. Back then, clerics were spiritual guides, arbiters of disputes, and judges of religious matters.

Janusz remembered that Iranians had first tried to implement a democratic constitution in 1906. Yet, after almost a century of struggle, they had gotten a new version of Islamic government called the *Velayat-e Faqih*—a system where the ultimate authority was vested in the most learned Islamic cleric whose official title was supreme leader. In 1979, for the first time in Iranian history, the reigning monarch was replaced by a cleric who had declared himself a representative of the Hidden Imam Mahdi. The new ruler didn't need a crown as a turban already covered his head. This system was the brainchild of Ayatollah Semnani, the founder of the Islamic Republic of Iran. He had called for the Shi'a priestly class to take a leading role in the day-to-day administration of state affairs. Unfortunately, for the average Iranian, Ayatollah Semnani and the clerics were just as brutal, if not more so, than the monarch they had replaced.

Ayatollah Semnani's vision to hasten the return of Imam Mahdi called for direct intervention in state affairs. Imam Mahdi, the Twelfth Shi'a Prophet, had disappeared at the age of five. He was considered to be in a state of occultation until a period of great upheaval that would facilitate his return to lead the believers. Many Shi'a scholars had explained that Islamic government should not be instituted until Imam Mahdi's return. They had explained that involvement in political affairs would corrupt religious institutions in the eyes of the masses. By manipulating the decisions of the kings, the clerics always had their say in political affairs while blaming the monarch for policies that were deemed to be ineffective. Direct involvement in politics had the disadvantage of eliminating the space between Mosque and State.

However, Ayatollah Semnani had greater ambitions than his supporters had imagined. He wanted to use the power of the Iranian state to spread Shi'a Islam to the far corners of the world. The most hardcore of his early followers included a group of men who had created an organization called the Office of Liberation Movements. This group would later be known as the Qods Force (QF), the external branch of the IRGC. These men implemented their vision after the downfall of the Shah by exporting their revolution to all regions of the Middle East with a Shi'a population. The QF had a presence in such places as Southern Lebanon, the Persian Gulf Arab Monarchies, and Iraq. In reality, it was this groups' provocation of Shi'a Iraqis in 1979 that forced Saddam Hussein to attack Iran in September of 1980 to put the Iranian revolutionaries on the defense.

The newly radicalized Iranians also had a hand in the creation of the Lebanese Hezbollah. This group was a more committed offshoot of the militant Amal Organization, created by the Iranian Shi'a cleric Musa Sadr in 1975. In fact, the victory of Ayatollah Semnani's supporters had so emboldened young Iranians that they worked around the clock to establish Hezbollah cells among Shi'a minorities on the Arab side of the Persian Gulf. All this activity was part of the struggle between the just and the unjust that Ayatollah Semnani believed characterized world affairs. The struggle would reach its crescendo with the arrival of Imam Mahdi to lead a decisive battle against the forces of evil. Ayatollah Semnani told his followers that the United States led the forces of evil in the modern world. It was therefore logical that Iran's foreign policy would be characterized by a struggle against the United States. Final victory would be declared only when Shi'a Iran defeated the Americans.

Given this reality, it would be difficult to deter the leaders of Islamic Iran. They didn't play by the traditional rules of nation states in the Westphalian system, characterized by the struggle to maintain sovereignty within defined borders. For Iranian radicals, the ultimate goal was the spread of Shi'a Islam around the world. Shi'ism was not just their religion; it was their political ideology.

13. THE GRAND HYATT HOTEL, KUALA LUMPUR, MALAYSIA

October 21

T he Grand Hyatt was considered one of the more luxurious hotels in Kuala Lumpur. Janusz had mistakenly answered his cell phone on the way to the hotel, prompting a longer than expected conversation with Jennifer. He was now anxious about arriving late to his rendezvous with the Iranian. It didn't help things that he had two hundred thousand dollars stashed in a money belt.

He took the elevator to the thirty-eighth-floor sky lobby with breathtaking views of the entire city. On his way up, he reassured himself that Iranians were rarely on time. Operational meetings always reminded him of the reasons the Unit was absolutely essential to America's security. The United States government had long ago lost its appetite for taking risks. There was now an army of lawyers at every level of the chain of command, from the National Security Council down to the operations offices of the various intelligence agencies. Their purpose was to ensure that every clandestine operation complied with international law without offending the sensibilities of media audiences around the globe. Operations were slowed down by the need to clear every minute detail with a government attorney. To top it all off, congressional oversight committees could cut funding for the operations based on a disagreement with the Executive Branch on unrelated matters. The result was a risk-averse Intelligence Community, unresponsive to rapidly emerging threats.

Conversely, the Unit was a private organization that didn't require the support or approval of any branch of the US government. Of course, there was cooperation with congress, but it was understood that the Unit would act whenever needed. Janusz was confident his superiors would never second-guess his decisions, allowing him to do whatever was necessary to neutralize threats as they evolved. Political Correctness was not something he had to worry about at the Unit. He was also not one to doubt his own core beliefs. He didn't enjoy killing, but he would not hesitate to do so if it meant saving American lives. Despite the argument of the liberals to the contrary, he was certain that the ideals of men such as James Madison needed to be protected even if that required the use of knives, guns, and bombs. America had enemies who wanted to do her harm. It was his job to get to them before they could act. Above all else, he believed he owed a debt to the wonderful country that had allowed his parents an opportunity to start a new life in a land where they didn't have to worry about their freedom.

He stepped out of the elevator at precisely five past seven and walked downstairs to the sky lounge. He strolled around for a few minutes, searching for his target. He wore a light disguise, exaggerating his eyebrows and nose, to mask his clean-shaven face. His tailored Italian suit accentuated his physique. He finally spotted the man he was after at a corner table.

Nasser was the only person seated at a round table with four chairs. He had a direct view of the Petronas Towers, considered the tallest building in the world not too long ago. Nasser was facing the Towers, his back toward Janusz.

"Nasser?"

Nasser stood up to shake hands with the American.

"Ah yes, you must be John. Derrick has told me about you."

Janusz preferred to use the English version of his given name. During his time at the CIA, he had used the name "John King" as his cover-for-action—a name used when a CIA case officer was pretending to be someone else for the purpose of a specific operation. He had chosen this cover name because it was a direct translation of his Polish first name and his Persian last name.

They shook hands before sitting across from each other as they gazed at the Towers. Nasser asked him if he wanted anything to drink. The Iranian was sipping a tall glass of mango juice, a local favorite.

"I'll have what you're having."

"Excellent choice. They have the best mango juice here." The evening crowd settled around them as Janusz steered the conversation to a more serious topic.

"I apologize that my colleagues were unable to get back to you sooner. Let me assure you that we're extremely interested in what you want to tell us about the IRGC and its missile program."

Nasser was visibly uncomfortable discussing the topic in the open. "Sir, are you sure you want to talk about this here?"

Janusz always made it a point to accommodate his sources to the extent possible. After all, they were the ones risking their lives. "Where do you suggest we go?"

"My room on the thirtieth floor is quite comfortable. I hope that's not a problem."

"That sounds good. Please lead the way."

They made their way to the elevators. Ten minutes later, Janusz and Nasser walked into room 3014. They headed toward a glass conference table surrounded by four leather swivel chairs. Janusz sat down while the Iranian headed for the minibar to get two cold bottles of water. Janusz grabbed one of the bottles. He waited for Nasser to sit across from him. However, the Iranian just stood there.

"Aren't you forgetting something, Mr. John?"

Janusz was not quite sure what Nasser was hinting about at first. Then it hit him. He unzipped his pants and placed the money belt on the table. He had been tempted to take some of the cash to play the local casinos. He had the option of making a temporary excuse before paying the asset at a later date. Janusz had always been a responsible gambler. Besides, what was the point of life if you didn't take risks every once in a while? It was not by choice that he'd fallen into this. The only downside was he'd promised his parents and Jennifer that he'd stopped gambling. Everyone in the world had some sort of vice. Betting provided him a rush, and it wasn't an issue that overly concerned him until recently.

"Here we are—two hundred thousand American dollars as promised for our initial meeting. You'll get the rest when we confirm you're providing accurate information."

Nasser shook his head before counting the money. He grabbed a bag from underneath the bed, placed the currency inside, then proceeded toward a closet next to the bed. The closet contained a safe deposit box where he secured the bag. Once Nasser was seated, he nervously took a sip of water. Janusz launched his questions.

"Okay, Nasser, what's your occupation? Please also explain your connection to the IRGC."

"I'm a sales representative for a trading company called Gulf Limited. We specialize in buying sanctioned items abroad for the Iranian market. Anytime you want to import goods to Iran, you need to get permission from the IRGC. The IRGC controls all ports of entry into the country. If you don't have a connection with them, then you must pay them off. I'm lucky in this regard. My wife has several family members who are high-ranking officers in the organization. One of her uncles happens to be an IRGC general. It is through him that I've become aware the IRGC has a new missile program."

Janusz took notes while simultaneously processing the source's information against his own knowledge. "What's the name of your wife's uncle? Please also provide his exact position in the IRGC?"

Nasser was now visibly uncomfortable. Swallowing hard, he took another sip of water before surrendering his reply. "I'm not sure I can give you this information, Mr. John. It was provided to me in confidence. I don't want to cause any problems for my family."

Janusz observed Nasser for a while. He didn't want to push him too hard, too fast. "What types of missiles is the IRGC working on? What are their ranges?"

Again, there was a blank expression on Nasser's face. He was clearly hesitant to cooperate. "Listen, Nasser, you're going to have to give me more than what your wife's uncle in the IRGC told you about a new missile program for two million dollars. I understand your hesitance to get your family in trouble, but I need more infor—" As Janusz was finishing his sentence, something hit the door from the hallway. Two seconds later, there was a second thud, followed by a third.

"Are you expecting someone, Nasser?" Janusz asked.

"I've no idea. Perhaps someone is searching for you, Mr. John?"

"Only one way to find out. I'll hide in the closet while you talk to whoever it is. I'll come out to assist you, if necessary."

As soon as Janusz was out of sight, the door flew open.

"So this is what you're up to when you're not at the office!" The man said.

Nasser was suddenly immersed in an out of body experience. He became a fly on the wall, observing himself from above. His face was drained of blood when the door flew open. The intruder was Javad Pirnia, his IRGC-IO minder. *Why the hell did Javad follow me*?

"So, you were sick tonight and wanted 'to go out for some fresh air before turning in.' You seemed to be having a good time with the man in the sky lobby," Javad said. "Care to provide an explanation?"

Nasser struggled to invent something to say. "Actually, it's quite simple," he finally mustered. "You'll probably understand why I don't want anyone to know about this." Nasser hesitated. "I … I've always had homosexual desires that I could not fulfill back home. Going outside the country is always a good opportunity to indulge my fantasies of having sex with American men."

Javad seemed to be taken aback by this startling revelation.

"Whether you're a faggot or a traitor is something for our brothers back home to determine. For now, you must accompany me. I'll need you to make a full confession about everything you've done toni—"

Before he could finish his sentence, Javad fell onto Nasser from a cold blow to the back of his head. The IRGC-IO man was quite resilient. He quickly turned and threw a jab at the American that landed in the air. John counterpunched him in his right kidney before grabbing him around the neck. The Iranian lowered his upper body to lift the American off the ground. He took a few steps back to slam the American against the bathroom door, hoping to shake him off. But the American was hard as nails. As he struggled to shake free, Javad was getting dizzy. He reached over to remove a knife holstered to his waist. John immediately tightened his grip until Javad's body went limp. He then pushed the body onto the bed. Nasser walked over to check for a pulse.

Nothing! Javad was definitely dead.

"What the hell did you do?"

"I think this solves your problem, Nasser. I don't know who this man is, but he won't be bothering you anymore."

"How am I going to explain this to the local authorities? This … This man's body is on my bed!"

"You don't have to explain anything. I'll have our people bring a large suitcase. We'll take care of the rest. I'll get back to you by tomorrow to arrange our next meeting."

"Why?"

"Because you need to take a polygraph and answer a few more of my questions. Remember, you didn't leave your room all night."

The American took out his phone and made the call. Within an hour, two men showed up in room 3014.

14. THE UNIT'S SAFE HOUSE, KUALA LUMPUR, MALAYSIA

October 22

I t didn't take Janusz long to contact the source for the follow-up meeting. The next day, Nasser slipped into a dark sedan that picked him up a few blocks away from the hotel. The drive to the suburbs of Kuala Lumpur went faster than expected. Nasser rode with Janusz in the back seat of the sedan with the tinted windows. The chauffeur finally pulled into the driveway of a large estate house in an upscale neighborhood. This was the Unit's safe house in Malaysia. Within minutes, the men were walking through a foyer and down a hallway. At the end of the hallway, there was an average-sized room with a chair in the middle that had several wires running to it. Nasser began fidgeting in place as soon as he entered the room.

"You seem nervous, Nasser. It's only a polygraph machine. Your cooperation with the US government will be rewarded as promised."

"No problem. Let's begin."

"I like your attitude!" Janusz replied.

Janusz and James Black, a technical expert, proceeded to connect Nasser to the polygraph machine. There were instruments to measure the heart rate, breathing, and perspiration. The machine's success was mostly due to the psychological effect it had on the subject connected to it. That was all that mattered to those who swore by its effectiveness. The first set of questions asked about a subject's name, place, and date of birth. These questions and a few others were meant to establish a baseline for the subject's normal rhythms.

"What's your full name?"

"Nasser Alitash."

"What is your profession?"

"I'm a representative of a trading company."

With the baseline questions out of the way, they proceeded to more serious matters.

"Does the IRGC have a new missile program?"

"Yes."

"What kind of missiles are they developing?"

"I don't know."

"Why does the IRGC need its own missile program when the Aerospace Industries Organization is the primary developer of missiles in Iran?"

"Because our Supreme Leader, Ayatollah Mashhadi, likes to keep his options open. He usually prefers a minimum of two organizations with the same function working in parallel on the same program. That is the way the Islamic Republic has functioned since its birth."

"And why is that?" Janusz asked.

"Because clerical representatives ensure that no officer can advance in rank without loyalty to the supreme leader and an appropriate level of religiosity. Are you starting to detect a pattern here, John? The Aerospace Industries Organization is under the direction of the Minister of Defense, which is a cabinet department, subordinate to the Office of the President. Even though the supreme leader is the commander and chief of the military, he feels he has more control over the activities run by the IRGC."

Janusz fell silent while taking notes. "Okay, Nasser. Why did you approach our embassy about the IRGC's new missile program?"

"Two reasons. First, I've always been a fan of the United States as a protector of freedom around the world. Second, I'm planning to take my family out of Iran to seek asylum in the

States. The money will be useful to help us establish a new life in your country."

"What about the other personalities in the program. Can you tell us anything about them? Who's in charge of what?"

"Well, the program is highly compartmented. My wife's uncle only told me generalities about a new missile program, nothing more. He'd never mention names, and I would not dare to ask either."

Something about Nasser's answers was rubbing Janusz the wrong way. Perhaps it was the tone of his replies or the constant shifting of his eyes around the room. Nasser was definitely trying to hide something. Janusz suddenly ended the session.

"Thank you for your time, Nasser. We'll contact you over the coming days after we've analyzed your replies."

When Nasser left, Janusz and James reviewed the results of the test. Twenty minutes later, James turned to Janusz.

"I hate to be the bearer of bad news, but this guy's answers are all over the place. The machine indicates deception in response to at least two questions."

"I don't need a machine to tell me this guy is fucking with us. I don't buy his story. The way I figure it, Nasser might himself be a part of the program."

When Nasser returned to his room at the Grand Hyatt, he had a sudden change of heart. He decided that he had gone as far as he could with the Americans. Most likely, they would realize that he'd lied to them, which only meant there was no way left for him to extort the remaining one point eight million dollars. He was also running the risk of being caught each time he met with them. He had foolishly directed the attention of the Americans to his country's clandestine missile program because he was angry. Even worse, Javad had been killed, and people were going to ask probing questions. All he had gotten for his troubles was a measly two hundred thousand dollars, a decent amount of money, but not enough for retirement. He needed to report the incident with John King in a way that would deflect attention from himself.

15. UNIT 81 HEADQUARTERS, HERNDON, VA

October 22

B ack in Herndon, Tom Stone, head of research and analysis, was briefing the Unit's senior members regarding the acquisition of Rostami Partners. In order to get a foothold in Iran, they needed access to the IRGC. Tom began his presentation with a short history of the IRGC. He supplemented this by providing a background on the personalities of some of its most important leaders. Finally, he revealed the places where most IRGC officials lived and the role they currently played in the Iranian economy. Tom explained the importance of the northeast Tehran region of Lavizan—the preferred neighborhood of high-ranking officials in the IRGC.

The IRGC was now the epicenter of all political, military, and economic activities in Iran. Their officers had come a long way since the early days of the revolution when most volunteers had emerged from the impoverished neighborhoods of South Tehran. They had been inspired by Ayatollah Semnani to defend the revolution, willing to give their lives for very little in return.

As the years passed, the IRGC slowly dug its heels into every segment of the economy. They now resembled the Russian mob. Anyone who wanted to do business in Iran had to pay a fee or risk a shakedown. When the disastrous war with Iraq ended in 1988, the government asked the IRGC to help rebuild the country with the equipment it had captured fighting the enemy. A decade later, every major infrastructure project in Iran was either contracted to the IRGC or managed by it.

The IRGC conglomerate, the *Khatam-al Anbiya Construction Headquarters*, was the largest firm of its kind in Iran. On rare occasions when Khatam lost a bid for a construction project, the IRGC had to be appeased by having one of its numerous subcontractors hired for a portion of the work. Like all bureaucracies around the world, the IRGC had developed numerous security units over the years to execute its duties. One such unit was responsible for the security of all airports and airplanes in Iran, placing the fox in charge of the hen house. This arrangement ensured that anyone interested in the business of importing or exporting goods across Iranian borders would pay their fair share to the IRGC godfathers. With the profits from these activities, the guards were able to invest in every sector of the Iranian economy. As a bonus, each time the government privatized a state-owned enterprise, a group of retired IRGC officers could buy the majority of shares at insider rates.

Most companies selling shares on the Tehran Stock Exchange were also under the control of retired IRGC officers. This reality effectively allowed the guards to manipulate prices on the Tehran Stock Exchange. It was perhaps more appropriate to change the name of this ancient country from Iran to IRGC-land. When Tom finished his sobering presentation, everyone turned to Tony.

"Aren't you excited to enter into business with our new Iranian partners?" Tony said mockingly. "I'm not sparing any expense to get access and insight into Iran. If we don't do it, the Intelligence Community sure as hell won't. Let's make this happen, people." The coming battle with the IRGC would be the most challenging problem that the Unit had tackled since its inception.

16. IRGC JOINT STAFF HEADQUARTERS, EASTERN TEHRAN, IRAN

October 24

C olonel Hadi Ramazani was nervous to barge into the boss's office unannounced. Most people who crossed the commander of the IRGC-IO ended up in excruciating pain, or they ended up dead. Colonel Ramazani knew better than anyone that the IRGC-IO was the most powerful security organ in the Islamic Republic of Iran. Actions threatening national security were one of the quickest ways to end up in its numerous detention centers.

The organization had been created to fight counter-revolutionaries. Over the years, it had accumulated new powers as its primary internal rival, the Ministry of Intelligence (MOIS), lost favor with the supreme leader. Many officials from the MOIS had gravitated toward the so-called reformist movement that opposed the ever-expanding powers of Ayatollah Mashhadi. The IRGC's intelligence organization was now the primary instrument of repression in Iran. It was not just the regime's opponents that could be rounded up. Anyone who opposed the supreme leader as the ultimate arbiter of power could end up in an IRGC prison.

The man the colonel was here to see, Katkhodah Lankarani, wore a white turban. He was a cleric who started his career in the MOIS before transferring to the Office of the Supreme Leader. He specialized in national intelligence matters. After gaining the trust of Ayatollah Mashhadi, Lankarani had been appointed director of the IRGC-IO. He had subsequently gained a reputation for dealing harshly with regime opponents who dared to speak their minds. Recently, he had started focusing the IRGC-IO's resources on the most insidious threat to national security—the threat posed to the supreme leader by those already entrenched inside the regime. These bad actors could be anyone in the government. The supreme leader called this group the "deviants." Lankarani had formed a special unit within the IRGC-IO to ferret out anyone suspected of this particular treason. Colonel Ramazani was now in charge of this effort with carte blanche to do whatever was necessary. Despite months of hard work and thousands of dollars spent establishing a network of informants, there was little to show for it.

At twenty past ten, Colonel Ramazani entered the boss's office holding a tan folder in his hand. The phrase "Top Secret" was stamped in red on the outside cover. "What is it? Can't you see I'm busy?" Lankarani growled at the decorated war veteran as though he were the office secretary.

"I thought you may want to read this report. I received it last night, sir."

"Unless you're here to tell me you've uncovered a high-ranking official in the government plotting to kill Ayatollah Mashhadi, I don't want to hear it."

The colonel, who, unbeknownst to Lankarani, was a first cousin of the supreme leader, spoke what was on his mind. His ties to Ayatollah Mashhadi were a secret miraculously hidden as he rose through the ranks. Colonel Ramazani's mother had "married" into the family through a *sigheh.* It was a temporary marriage never acknowledged publicly.

"If victories against our enemies came that easily, there would be no need for an organization such as this. As I briefed you last week, the director of the Buraq Project has sent several of his top experts to the Far East on a secret mission."

Lankarani rolled his eyes, visibly annoyed. Colonel Ramazani continued as before, not letting his boss intimidate him. The name of the game in Iran was connections. If you had connections with the highest echelons of power, it meant that you were protected without worry about such trivial matters as upsetting your superior in the formal chain of command. That was only an issue in countries where officials derived power from their positions as opposed to their connections.

"As is to be expected for a sensitive mission such as this, the team that departed for the Far East was accompanied by two of our intelligence operatives. One is an overt agent of this organization. The other is a paid asset of the IRGC-IO, posing as a propulsion engineer."

"Why are you telling me all this?" Lankarani demanded by raising his voice.

"I'm getting there, sir. I've just been informed that they have not heard from our overt officer in Kuala Lumpur, Javad Pirnia, in three days. This is most unusual because our people are not allowed to be out of contact for this long."

"Why is this important?"

"Because the head of the delegation has reported that an American has approached him. The American gave this man, Massoud Hosseinzadeh, his business card for future contact."

The colonel finally had Lankarani's complete attention.

"Send a team out to Kuala Lumpur to dig around. Keep me informed of every step and have them keep tabs on the American. Don't hesitate to get rid of him if necessary."

It was obvious that his boss was not fit to run a shoe store much less the premier intelligence agency of the Islamic Iran. Pity that Lankarani was also a classmate of Ayatollah Mashhadi in the Qom Seminary. It would have been much easier to get rid of him otherwise.

17. THE GRAND HYATT HOTEL, KUALA LUMPUR, MALAYSIA

October 27

The two teams had been keeping track of the source's movements all week. Nasser stayed at his hotel on most days, venturing out occasionally. Janusz decided to take the risk. There was no way to find out about Nasser unless they broke into his room at the Grand Hyatt.

The team split in two. Ed Wright, Phantom Two, was going to monitor Nasser when he left the hotel. Janusz, Eric Bradford, and James Black were Phantom One. Their job was to enter Nasser's room to recover available intelligence. The call finally came through Janusz's earpiece.

"Phantom One, this is Phantom Two, do you read?"

"Phantom Two, read you loud and clear."

"The subject is on the move. He just exited the garage driveway."

"Copy that."

Janusz turned toward the others, "Okay, Nasser just left the hotel. James, do you have everything you need?"

"Yup! I paid a hotel employee a hundred bucks for a key to his room. Don't need much else."

"Right! Let's go!"

When the elevator reached the thirtieth floor, they headed straight to room 3014. James inserted the key into the slot. A blinking green light appeared.

"Bingo! After you, gentlemen," James said. They searched every nook and cranny for clues. They took great care to ensure that nothing seemed out of place when Nasser returned. They finally found a brown leather briefcase under a pile of clothes. Janusz brought it to the conference table to empty its contents. There were numerous documents written in Farsi. Some of them had the word "*seri*," the Farsi word for *secret*, written at the top.

"I can't believe this!"

"What is it, Janusz?" Eric said.

"This guy has classified IRGC documents in his briefcase. Why would a representative of—" Janusz said.

"What does it say?"

"Give me a few seconds here, Eric. In the meantime, take pictures of all the other documents on the table."

Just as Janusz was giving these instructions, James came back with several memory sticks in his hand and an inquisitive look in his eye.

"Start downloading their contents onto the portable hard drive. We're not taking anything with us!" Janusz said.

As the others were busy taking pictures of various documents in the room, Janusz suddenly shouted out, "Jesus Christ! I knew this son of a bitch was playing us for fools! His name is not Nasser. It's Massoud Hosseinzadeh. He is a representative of Gulf Limited LLC as he told us, and he's here to procure fuel for a project, code-named Buraq."

At that moment, Janusz's earpiece came to life. "Phantom One, this is Phantom Two. You need to get out of there, pronto. Subject is on the move."

"What do you mean 'on the move'? Where is he exactly?" Janusz said.

"He's about to turn his car over to the valet. He should be up in the next five minutes."

"Fuck! We've got to go!" Janusz said.

"But we haven't downloaded all the files yet. Plus, I was

hoping to break into that safe in his closet to get our two hundred thousand back." James said.

"Forget the money and the rest of the files, James. We have less than five minutes to get this place back to the way it was when we walked in." The team put away the thumb drives and documents as fast as they could, hoping nothing was out of place.

Janusz quickly turned the rest of the pages to memorize the contents of the file. They tidied up the room before making their way to the door. The door to the elevator carrying Massoud Hosseinzadeh opened precisely at the moment the three men were about to step outside into the hall. The bank of elevators was no more than twenty feet down the hall around a corner. When they stepped outside room 3014, the elevator doors opened.

"Fuck. He's here," Janusz said, closing the door behind them. They stood in the hallway in search of an escape. Janusz searched down the hall in the other direction. Next to an open room was a cleaning cart.

"Let's go in there."

The others followed Janusz inside. Fortunately, the maid was in the restroom. They stood by the front door, listening to the approaching footsteps. Janusz's earpiece came to life again.

"Phantom One, what's your status? I repeat, what's your status?"

Janusz mouthed the word "fuck" as he turned off his communications gear. Would the maid come out to check the noise? A door slammed shut outside. James peered out into the hallway.

"The coast is clear," he said.

"Let's go!" Janusz replied.

They moved out of the room 3020 and walked down the hallway without the maid ever knowing they had been there. They finally made it to the elevator. Janusz anxiously pressed the button. The next forty-five seconds seemed closer to five minutes as they stood without cover. The doors finally opened.

On their way down, Janusz laughed out loud. "I'm going to kill Ed when I get my hands on him."

Numerous questions required immediate answers. The most important was the status of project Buraq and its intended target.

18. THE EMBASSY OF THE ISLAMIC REPUBLIC OF IRAN, KUALA LUMPUR, MALAYSIA

October 27

After a thirty-minute delay at customs, Saman Shoosh-tari and Asghar Tavakoli drove to the Iranian Embassy in Kuala Lumpur. They rented a Toyota RAV 4 SUV using the cover names under which the Iranian government had issued their passports. Upon arriving at the embassy compound, they went straight to the attaché's office. An IRGC naval officer informed them that Massoud Hosseinzadeh had not yet arrived for work. They departed without further explanation. Within minutes, they were on the road toward the Grand Hyatt in Kuala Lumpur. Saman had been an advisor to Shi'a militias in Iraq during the early part of the American occupation. His Iraqi liaisons in the "special groups" were told that Saman was an officer of the IRGC QF on assignment to train them in urban warfare. In reality, Saman was a QF Counter Intelligence (CI) officer with a mandate to teach CI elements in the Iraqi Mahdi Army and the Badr Corps how to conduct interrogations of captured enemy forces. Interrogations were Saman's specialty.

There were very few in the IRGC who could break the morale of a hostile subject faster than he could. His partner, Asghar, was previously a QF advisor before transferring to the IRGC-IO in anticipation of a promotion. Asghar wore his beard similarly to Saman, but he had less hair on his head as he was beginning to bald. Asghar had spent the majority of his QF career in South Lebanon as an advisor to the Lebanese Hezbollah group. He had helped them plan operations against Israel.

Asghar had also been a QF CI officer who specialized in interrogations. He had perfected a variety of torture techniques designed to make the toughest men give up their own mothers. The promise of career progression had lured both men to the intelligence organization of the IRGC. Their previous experience had brought them to the attention of Colonel Ramazani.

Inside the SUV, music by Andy, an Iranian pop singer from Los Angeles, was booming. This was perhaps an unusual choice for two devout followers of an Islamic theocracy, but Iran was a country full of contradictions.

Asghar suddenly spoke up. "Saman, I don't think it's a good idea for both of us to go up to Massoud's room together. I'll wait in the car while you go up for a chat with this guy."

Saman nodded to his superior. When they arrived, he opened the door. As he was getting out of the car, Asghar held on to his left arm.

"Wait. What do you make of that?" Asghar said.

"Three guys getting into a car?"

"Three guys getting into a car, one of whom fits the description provided by Massoud."

"Asghar, do you want me to have a talk with Massoud or not?"

"Forget about Massoud for now. We can talk to him later. We should follow this car where it leads us."

Saman nodded once more, and they were off. Forty minutes later, they found themselves in front of a large estate house on the outskirts of the city. They parked a block away and waited.

"I have a feeling that these guys are involved with the American the boss wants us to investigate. Let's run these plates with our contacts in the Kuala Lumpur city government. We'll stake this house out for as long as necessary. First, we must return to the embassy to grab our surveillance equipment."

Two hours later, they were back at the Grand Hyatt. This

time, Asghar decided to chat with Massoud by himself.

The pounding on the door was déjà vu. Massoud was not expecting guests. His immediate thought was that the American had returned to pay him a visit. "Give me a second to get dressed. I was in the shower." Massoud yelled out in English.

"*Daro Vaz kon, as tarafe Sefarat oomadam.*" The man outside said he was from the embassy. Massoud knew right away that he was most likely with the IRGC, here to investigate the disappearance of Javad. Massoud quickly grabbed an undershirt and a pair of boxers before opening the door.

"*In che vazeshe*? Why did you come to the door without your pants? Are you playing with yourself when you should be at work for the Iranian government?" Massoud took note of the visitor's size, quickly reminding himself that he was on his own this time.

"I'm sorry. I was in the shower. I didn't mean to keep you waiting. Please take a seat. I'll be with you momentarily." As soon as he returned, his guest peppered him with questions.

"Massoud Hosseinzadeh?"

"Yes, with whom do I have the pleasure of speaking?"

"Call me Asghar. I'm here to talk to you about a colleague, Javad Pirnia."

"Is everything alright? I've not seen him for a few days. I assumed he went back to Tehran."

"That's what I'm here to find out. When was the last time you spoke with him?"

"I believe it was the evening of the twenty-first. I was sick that night and decided to stay in. He came by my room around eight in the evening if I am not mistaken."

"What happened next?"

"He wanted to make sure I was okay. I told him I needed to rest after thanking him for checking up on me. That was the last time I spoke with him."

"What exactly did he say to you that evening?"

"Nothing. He just wanted to know how I was doing. I was not really in the mood for small talk, and neither was he."

"I'm going to level with you, Massoud. No one has heard from Javad since he visited you. That is what brings me here to your room."

"I'll state for the record that I'll cooperate with your investigation in any way that I can."

"If what you've just told me is an accurate description of the events, then I have nothing further for you at this time. Here's my business card. I'll remain in Malaysia while I conduct my investigation. Thank you for your cooperation."

As Asghar closed the door behind him, Massoud's problems were just beginning. He pictured himself being taken to a cell in Evin prison where he would be tied and beaten with cables on the soles of his feet. After several days of torture, he imagined himself begging to be put out of his misery. He considered calling John King to ask for an immediate extraction to America. But then, that would ruin his chances of leading the missile program. His best option was to procure an energetic missile fuel from the Chinese. Then he could leverage his status as a hero to clear his name. Massoud took his wallet and his room key. He needed several shots of whiskey to take the edge off. He would not be able to drink as freely in front of friends and relatives back home.

19. BOARDING THE GULFSTREAM, KUALA LUMPUR, MALAYSIA

October 29

T he beauty of traveling the globe on the Gulfstream G650 was that no time or energy was wasted going through security checks like the rest of the flying public. The chauffeur drove the limousine to a restricted part of the tarmac and dropped Janusz in front of the plane. The driver then loaded his luggage into the underbelly of the metal bird as Janusz climbed a short staircase into the main cabin. The inside was furnished with plush leather sofas and chairs. There was an assortment of luxury items for his exclusive use, a perk usually reserved for corporate CEOs. The seats were made of hand-stitched leather, the cabinets of mahogany wood. A fully stocked bar complemented the setting. There was even a bedroom with a king-sized bed, pillow-top mattresses, satin sheets, and a private shower.

World-class meals were integral to the service. Janusz had a choice of either fresh-caught salmon with saffron rice or filet mignon with asparagus. This was preceded by Maine lobster and Beluga caviar. For dessert, he could choose either a decadent opera cake or a sinful slice of chocolate cake with vanilla ice cream. Tony had spared no expense as usual.

As he reclined in his seat, Janusz recalled his first mission on behalf of the Unit. The QF had gathered its best Shi'a foot soldiers from the Lebanese Hezbollah and the Iraqi Ansar Al Haq. The selected warriors had been sent to several covert training camps in Iran where they'd trained in the art of surveillance, kidnapping, and assassination. When they had completed their training, the specialists were sent to kill American soldiers stationed outside of war zones, where they least expected to be attacked.

The IRGC proxies had planned the murders to appear as the work of Sunni extremists, such as Al Qaeda. The men sent to Europe had been trained to target American soldiers in order to disable their vehicles, causing fatal car accidents. The key to success had been to ensure that all the operatives escaped the area, avoiding interrogations that could reveal their connection to Iran. After several days, Janusz had tracked down the source of the information to confirm the veracity of the story. He then traveled to Germany to find the assassins, playing the part of an American soldier.

A week later, Janusz had discovered the location of all five men in Stuttgart. He entered their safe house one night, killing three in their beds. The other two had put up a fight, which made things more interesting. He slit Ali's throat using an *Ansar al Haq* inscribed knife, likely meant to kill Americans. Hassan was with Hezbollah, and he'd almost gotten the best of Janusz. Janusz snapped his neck—but not before staring into his eyes while saying, in Arabic, "This is for the Americans you intended to kill, you son of bitch."

On this particular trip, Janusz was on his way to meet a friend in Iceland. Johan Olafsson, an arms dealer he had met years earlier, was able to procure anything for anyone. Johan was part of the new generation of enterprising Icelanders who had adopted the American drive to get rich. It was Johan who had first introduced Janusz to the glamorous world of horse racing. He'd immediately used that knowledge to make some extra money. Johan had made his way to Turkey in his early twenties. He ended up as a bouncer, making the rounds at the Istanbul dance clubs. It was through the clubs that he'd met a group of Turks who showed him how much money could be made smuggling weapons to war zones from Grozny to Sarajevo and everywhere in between. His people skills and his ability to learn any language in record time had helped Johan make friends on every continent.

It did not take long for the CIA to start using Johan as one of their conduits for conflicts where the role of the US Government was to remain hidden. Johan had started out smuggling small arms but was soon acting as the CIA's intermediary for larger weapon systems. When Russia's SVR became aware of his talents, they too retained Johan. Once the Iranians heard of Johan's connections, they had inquired about his ability to obtain parts for nuclear weapons. He had turned them down, but over time, Johan had cultivated extensive ties with the IRGC. The Iranians were always in the market for foreign-made weapons, especially those made by their primary adversary, the Americans. Johan and Janusz had cultivated a rather warm relationship over the years. Janusz had a way of putting people at ease, and Johan rarely said no to his request for a meeting.

After leaving the CIA, Janusz had told him that he was working for a private equity firm that did a fair amount of business with front companies that procured weapons for Middle Eastern states. It was only natural for them to compare notes about customers in the arms trade. During their last conversation, Janusz had informed Johan that there was an urgent matter that required them to meet in person. Hesitant to discuss the topic over the phone, he had asked Johan about a company registered in Dubai under the name of Gulf Limited LLC. Johan agreed that it would be best for them to discuss the matter face-to-face.

The Gulfstream landed at Keflavik International Airport a quarter past 1:00 p.m. It was a pity that there was little time to ice climb on this trip. Iceland had several large glaciers perfect for such activities. The days were much shorter this time of year. He needed to get to the northern town of Akureyri before an impending blizzard closed the roads. To add to the danger, many of the bridges in that part of Iceland narrowed to only one lane. In a previous trip to northern Iceland, Janusz had driven through an evening blizzard and nearly smashed straight into an eighteen-wheel truck—a wall of snow had diminished visibility over the hood of the SUV on a one-lane bridge.

A crewmember opened the door for him to exit the plane. A brand new Range Rover was waiting on the tarmac. The local contact handed him the keys.

"Here you go, sir. The car is all fueled up and ready to go. Just be careful if you are headed toward the northern part of the island today. We're expecting a heavy blizzard."

"Yes, I'll be fine. Thanks for your help."

Janusz made a call to let Johan know he was on his way. "With any luck, I should be in Akureyri by 8:00 tonight."

"Don't push your luck, old boy. The storm headed our way is no joke, but knowing you, I expect to see you sooner. I'll keep your food warm."

"What are we having for dinner anyway?"

"A local specialty, Icelandic lamb."

"Perfect!"

Janusz wished that Johan hadn't mentioned the lamb. His stomach growled within the first hour of the drive. It didn't take long for the blizzard to pound his vehicle. It started out with a few flakes. Two hours later, he thought the wind would blow the SUV off the highway. Janusz pulled to the side of the road to let the worst pass. By the time he started driving again, it was 9:30 p.m. He had another forty kilometers to go. If he were lucky, he could reach Akureyri before midnight, and that meant he would be late for the lamb dinner. When he arrived, the town was deserted.

It was now 11:00 p.m. He passed by the lake and made his way to the winding desolate road. As he reached the end of the trail, Johan's darkened house was visible at a distance. Something didn't seem quite right. Instinct warned him to approach the house cautiously. Janusz grabbed his night-vision binoculars before turning to step outside. He tried opening the door. It was no use, he was trapped.

20. POLITICAL IDEOLOGICAL DIRECTORATE HEADQUARTERS OF THE GENERAL STAFF, CENTRAL TEHRAN, IRAN

October 29

Yadollah Boroujerdi was a devoted follower of the late Ayatollah Semnani. He considered himself one of the most ardent supporters of Velayat-e Faqih. Not long after Ayatollah Mashhadi's appointment as the new supreme leader, Boroujerdi helped him to consolidate power at the expense of the other factions in the regime. The new supreme leader didn't tolerate dissenting opinions among the clerical class as had his predecessor. Boroujerdi worried that a lack of tolerance would move the regime further away from the path of Imam Mahdi. Fortunately, Boroujerdi was a leading advocate of the effort to establish clerical control over the military. As a matter of fact, he had been appointed as the first director of the office to oversee ideological conformity in the military during the early days of the revolution.

As the IRGC became the favored security institution within the system, Boroujerdi was once again appointed to head Islamic indoctrination efforts in the Armed Forces General Staff, the organization created to coordinate activities between the regular military (the *Artesh*), and the IRGC. Thus, events had positioned him perfectly for what was about to unfold. Boroujerdi's office was on the top floor of the Armed Forces General Staff Headquarters on Ghoddoosi Street. It was neither the largest nor the most ostentatious room in the building. Those offices were reserved for general officers of the IRGC high command. In this particular case, however, the size of the office didn't reflect the importance of its occupant. The Political Ideological Directorate (PID) in the armed forces had come about because Ayatollah Semnani didn't trust the military he had inherited from the late Shah. Despite calls by the revolutionaries to disband the military, Ayatollah Semnani argued it would be foolish to do so, given the threats posed by regional enemies. The best solution that Ayatollah Semnani and his advisors in the Revolutionary Council came up with was to place clerical representatives at various echelons of the military.

What had begun as a haphazard effort to ensure clerical control had grown into a vast government bureaucracy that permeated every branch of the Iranian Armed Forces. Over the years, the ideological representatives of the supreme leader had multiplied. They were in charge of placing subordinate clerics at every level of the Armed Forces from the joint staff headquarters to individual air, ground, and naval units. It was now impossible for men in military uniform to advance without the consent of their devout overseers. Boroujerdi's men spent a considerable amount of time with the military as part of team-building exercises that included praying in groups five times a day.

This morning, Boroujerdi was reviewing a report he would present to Ayatollah Mashhadi later that day. He was reading when his assistant delivered a large tray with hot tea, pastries, and dates. He set the report aside to slowly sip his tea while munching on a date. It didn't take long before his cell phone rang. He was in no mood to take the call.

"Good morning, Mr. President. How are you?" Boroujerdi said.

"Never mind how I am. How are you coming along with your work?"

"Funny you should ask, I was just reviewing a report. The IRGC-IO has formed a special unit to gather information on the so-called deviants in our government. Colonel Hadi Ramazani heads this unit. It's been several days since they've heard from one of Ramazani's men accompanying the missile team in Malaysia. They're in a state of panic."

"What does that mean for us?" President Azari said.

Boroujerdi was rapidly coming to the conclusion that President Azari was a dimwit, in addition to being annoying.

"I'm not sure what this particular incident means for us, perhaps nothing. But that's beside the point. The fact is I'm aware of the most sensitive cases being investigated within the regime, and there is no indication that our plans are under scrutiny at this time. However, if Ramazani's men start sniffing around, I have the power to delay their investigations." Boroujerdi put his feet on the desk before stating with pride, "The beauty of my official power is that it allows me to observe the very people who are tasked with investigating us. Rather ironic, don't you think?"

"Yes, it's ironic indeed. Now make sure you're on top of Colonel Ramazani's men so they don't crash our party at the wrong time."

Boroujerdi shifted uneasily in his seat before breathing out. "I appreciate your reminders as always, Mr. President. Have a good day." Boroujerdi reminded himself that the idiot President Azari would quickly become irrelevant once he had served his purpose of hastening the return of Imam Mahdi.

21. JOHAN'S HOME, AKUREYRI, ICELAND

October 29

Despite using all his might to push the damn thing open, the driver-side door would not budge. The blizzard had covered the exterior of the vehicle with a solid sheet of ice. Janusz moved over to the passenger side. That door was jammed too. He jiggled the door open just enough for his next maneuver. He lay flat across the driver's seat with his feet pointing toward the passenger door. Several heavy kicks and the door flew open. It had finally stopped snowing, but it was pitch dark. As soon as he stepped out, Janusz found himself knee-deep in snow.

The silence was broken intermittently by the howls of the frigid wind. The combination of cold and wind sent a shiver down his spine. He fastened the night-vision binoculars against his face. Something was definitely not right. There were no lights on in Johan's house. What the hell could have happened? Was Johan already asleep? Was there an emergency that had forced him to go back into town? Wouldn't Johan call to leave a message? Perhaps the cell towers were down. He checked his own cell phone. There seemed to be no reception at the moment. As uninviting as the house appeared, he had no choice but to enter. He had flown seven thousand miles and driven through a blizzard to talk to Johan about Massoud Hosseinzadeh. He was not about to go back empty-handed.

Janusz climbed into the Range Rover and drove through

the snow. When he was a hundred feet from the front entrance, he turned off the engine. He sat in silence for about ten minutes, looking through the night-vision scope once again for signs of life. The thermometer in the car indicated it was -15 Celsius outside. When the dashboard clock next to the thermometer hit 11:15 p.m., Janusz decided to move. From below his seat, he picked up a small metal briefcase. Inside was a Sig Sauer MPX 9mm close-quarters combat weapon along with a silencer. In the glove compartment was a Sig Sauer 226 pistol, which Janusz put in his coat pocket. He then secured his night-vision goggles before breathing out. It was time to greet the cold. He exited the vehicle, headed toward the front of the house. Unlocking the safety, he switched the SIG MPX to burst mode. His instincts told him it was unwise to ring the bell.

He turned the knob to enter, but the door was locked. There was no choice now but to make a hard entry. Janusz put several rounds through the door handle. The suppressed shots broke the lock. He pushed the door wide open before walking into the foyer. Inside, the house was much colder than he had expected. He made his way carefully through the kitchen, taking great pains to remain silent. Johan had made more than a few enemies over the years in the underground arms trade. But what was the chance of his past catching up with him on the same night that Janusz came to visit?

He stepped out of the kitchen into the main hallway and walked down the passage toward a set of doors. He had visited Johan once before in this house, and he was beginning to remember his way around. He carefully opened a door on his right. He was certain that this was Johan's study the last time he had visited. When it opened, the door squealed. Against the silence of the empty house, it sounded like a loud shriek. *Why is Johan not oiling his door hinges?* He took a quick glance around the room, suddenly freezing in place.

There were numerous documents scattered on top of Johan's desk. The books on his shelf were haphazardly placed. That the study was in a state of disarray was unusual, to say the least. One of the most obvious characteristics of Johan was his attention to detail. It was evident in everything he did. Someone other than Johan had definitely been in this house. The question was whether they were still there. This realization brought Janusz's index finger a bit closer to the trigger. Despite the frost in the house, beads of sweat ran down his forehead and along the back of his neck. He reconsidered his reasons for remaining in Johan's house.

Perhaps it was best just to leave. He could reach out to his friend later. If this situation was the result of a weapons deal gone bad, it was not Janusz's fight. But Johan had always been fair in his dealings with him. If Johan were in trouble, Janusz could not just walk away. He decided that he would clear the house by walking through every room. He would search for clues as to what had happened to Johan. Even if his friend had been taken to another location, Janusz was now determined to get him back. He walked back out into the main hallway, proceeding methodically through each room. When he cleared the lower floor, he went upstairs to the bedrooms.

Nothing seemed unusual there, so he walked back down. He was growing concerned that the intruders had not left any clues. He suddenly remembered that there was one room in the house that he had not yet searched, the main dining room on the opposite end. His assault rifle was perched up against his face, ready to fire. When he reached the entryway to the dining room, he stopped dead in his tracks. With one quick motion, he swung his body around and stepped in. His reflex wanted to fire at the person sitting in the middle of the table, but somehow he was able to pull back.

Janusz spent the next thirty seconds frozen in his tracks as he stared at the figure in the center chair of the long dining table. There was something wrong; the figure was upright and motionless despite Janusz's presence in the room. He walked slowly toward the table, holding his index finger over the trigger, ready to fire at the slightest provocation. As he got closer, his heart sank in recognition that he was standing next to a dead body.

Johan was tied to the chair. His neck had been cut from ear to ear. There was a huge gash in the center of his throat. His mouth was slightly open with visible signs of trauma. Janusz lowered his weapon slightly, opening Johan's mouth to check inside. For some odd reason, the tongue was missing. He stared at the plate in front of Johan. A sharp knife and fork had been placed neatly on either side. A small piece of meat was resting in the middle of the plate. *Jesus Christ, that's Johan's tongue.* Whoever had staged this macabre scene had a big ax to grind with Johan and a seriously warped sense of humor.

Two men stood in the snow no more than fifty yards from the east side of the house. One of them dropped the cigarette from his mouth when the red light on the remote control blinked. The motion sensor they had placed inside the house had been triggered. He turned to his companion.

"Chikar konam?" What should I do, he blurted out.

"Yani Chi Chi kar konam. Dokma ro feshar bedeh digeh." *What do you mean what should I do. Press the button already.*

22. OFFICE OF SUPREME LEADER MASHHADI, CENTRAL TEHRAN, IRAN

October 29

A zerbaijan Street was neither the fanciest nor the most architecturally distinct in Tehran. Ayatollah Mashhadi had fallen in love with a property on this street as the location for his house and office years ago. The supreme leader of Iran began his day at 5 a.m. with the ritual morning prayer. By 6 a.m., he was sitting in the study of his house, reading reports on the state of affairs of the country of eighty million over which he exercised ultimate authority. 8 to 9 a.m. was reserved for breakfast with senior advisors to discuss the myriad problems of the government.

Ayatollah Mashhadi was of average height with a medium build. His hair had turned white years ago. In many ways, he resembled the countless Shi'a clerics with his cream overall manteaux, black cape, and a black turban. The color of his turban indicated direct descent from the family of Prophet Mohammad. Ayatollah Mashhadi's state-controlled media was always busy dispelling rumors that he was power-hungry. They knew better than to broadcast images of the supreme leader wearing his fancy jewelry or driving around in expensive cars. In an effort to disseminate the truth, the state media in post-revolutionary Iran, known as the Islamic Republic of Iran Broadcasting (IRIB), was managed by one of his representatives.

Ayatollah Mashhadi's house was located right next to the Presidential Palace. The offices of the Judiciary, the Guardian

Council, and the Expediency Council were on the same block. All these institutions were located near the former Shah's Marble Palace. Paradoxically, this concentrated center of power provided an easy target for the Americans if they ever chose to attack his regime. The supreme leader had always been more concerned with intrigue from within his own regime as opposed to a decapitation strike by an external power. This arrangement allowed him to keep tabs on all the major power players in Iran. The *Vali-e Amr* and *Ansar Al-Mahdi* Units of the IRGC, both answerable to him, provided security for the entire neighborhood.

Inside his compound, Ayatollah Mashhadi maintained a manicured garden where he strolled while pondering the affairs of state with a pipe in his mouth. The main house contained a collection of Iranian artwork consolidated from the palaces of the Shah or bought at art auctions. No reporter was ever allowed inside the residence, nor would his censors allow pictures from his home to be printed for the public. He had an extensive collection of valuable prayer beads, including several adorned with emeralds. The house contained many rare Persian rugs, purchased from foreign collectors. The entire collection was worth millions of dollars. At 2:00 p.m. it was time for a scheduled a meeting.

His interlocutor was the director of the IRGC-IO. Lately, the supreme leader was preoccupied with the idea that other men of influence within the regime wanted to eliminate his privileged position in the system. He had countered their moves by encouraging IRGC involvement in economic and political affairs in exchange for their promise to crush dissent.

Katkhodah arrived in time to give the supreme leader an afternoon briefing. After spending the first five minutes praising his boss, the IRGC-IO director launched into a diatribe.

"Sir, several of the senior clerics in Qom have been giving sermons questioning the legitimacy of your role as the supreme leader. Since it's not prudent to arrest these individuals, we requested that our brothers in *Ansar-e Hezbollah* disrupt their sermons by shouting in the audience every few minutes. Our agitators also initiated fights during their sermons, threatening to attack their supporters. As usual, this was enough to bring an early end to the gathering." The *Ansar-e Hezbollah* was the regime's unofficial vigilante group made up of former members of the IRGC who were paid to attack anyone seeking to "reform" the Islamic Republic or challenge the authority of Ayatollah Mashhadi.

"During the past week, we detained three of President Azari's advisors who had spoken around the world about the need for an eventual détente between the Islamic Republic and the USA. As these actions were taken without consultation with your office, our people admonished them that next time they would end up in Evin prison." Ayatollah Mashhadi didn't say much. He nodded his head occasionally to express approval of what he had heard.

"Before I finish, I want to bring to your attention two incidents we're investigating. The first is a recent meeting between President Azari, the defense minister, and the commanders of the IRGC at the presidential compound."

Ayatollah Mashhadi jumped in before Katkhodah could provide the details. "Stop right there. Don't waste your time examining this issue any further. My personal representative to the IRGC, Ayatollah Boroujerdi, was present. He already informed me that the president had called this meeting to express his support for our secret missile program. For once, I'm glad that the Office of the President is working to support my agenda. What's the second item you want to tell me about?"

"It's about the procurement team in East Asia."

"Yes, the director is a great man and a personal friend. We must give him all the support he needs."

"Well, sir, the problem is one of my men who was accompanying the team has disappeared. He has not been in contact for a while."

"So, what do you want me to do about that?"

"Nothing, I just wanted to inform you that we've sent a

team to investigate the matter. It's possible that either the Israelis or the Americans have taken our man. The problem is that if we assume the mission has been compromised, we must also assume that the other members of the team are in danger. Our enemies may try to kidnap the delegation head, Dr. Massoud Hosseinzadeh, or one of his assistants."

"How do we know your man hasn't defected? Perhaps he is the one who is compromising our efforts abroad. If that turns out to be the case, I'll hold you personally responsible for any delays in the missile program."

"We'll get to the bottom of this at once, sir. I can assure you that my people will never divulge information to the enemy even if their lives are in danger."

"I hope that turns out to be true in this case as well," Ayatollah Mashhadi said. The supreme leader dismissed his intelligence director with a wave of his hand. It was time for a nap.

23. JOHAN'S HOME, AKUREYRI, ICELAND

October 29

The blinking red light in the darkness outside the house prompted Janusz to run through the window. He jumped out headfirst into the snow and ran as fast as he could. Ten seconds later, the shockwave of the explosion knocked him to the ground. Either he had gone crazy or there were school bells ringing all around. The force of the blast had blown off the entire side of the house where Johan's dining room was located. Upon regaining his balance, Janusz saw two men running through the snow about sixty yards away. He had left the SIG MPX on the dining room table. He immediately reached for his coat pocket. Fortunately, the SIG 226 pistol was still there. He grabbed it, removing the safety before running after the men. His night vision goggles were still functional. The targets rushed toward a pair of snowmobiles parked nearby. Within seconds, they jumped on their getaway vehicles. After a short chase, Janusz stopped running and tried to remember where he had spotted their original location with the blinking red light. He finally found their footprints in the snow. He followed the trail, moving in the opposite direction from the snowmobiles.

He arrived at a point where the prints came to an end. It was obvious the intruders had spent some time here—they'd disturbed the snow. But what were they doing? Janusz remained at that spot for a few minutes carefully sifting through the snow for clues. Just as he was about to give up, he stepped on something hard. He took off his gloves, bending over to examine the snow with his bare hands. The metallic object stuck to his skin.

He examined the familiar object for a few seconds. His entire body cringed reflexively as all his muscles tightened. In their haste to leave the scene, one of the men had dropped his metal cigarette lighter. But this was not just any ordinary lighter. He had found the same type once before, outside of Baghdad. On another occasion, he had found one in Beirut. Both times, Janusz had taken the lighters out of the pockets of dead QF officers. He had killed the first man by putting a bullet in his skull and strangled the second. The lighters were etched with the IRGC logo, an extended arm holding a Kalashnikov rifle. They were issued to QF officers. The QF usually gifted them to trusted liaisons in proxy organizations such as the Lebanese Hezbollah. Janusz put the trophy in his pocket. This was the third such lighter he had captured from the QF. He should have killed at least one of them to earn it.

The way he considered it—the fewer of these terrorists walking on the earth, the better. But how had the IRGC known he was meeting with Johan tonight? Was it possible they were not here for Johan? If they were, they would have just killed him and fled the scene of the crime as quickly as possible. This particular trap must have been laid out just for Janusz. The only question was whether the IRGC believed they got their man or knew Janusz had escaped. He pondered the implications of the original question. How had the IRGC been able to find out that he would be Iceland at a certain time? Numerous measures were in place to protect operational security at headquarters, so any lapse must have happened out in the field. A call had to be made to the team in Kuala Lumpur to warn them about the possible security breach. Janusz spent the drive back to Keflavik International Airport reviewing options for access into the Iranian missile program.

The Gulfstream took off before sunrise, returning to Melbourne. He sent a coded distress message to Kuala Lumpur and slept for the next nine hours. When he awakened, he made a secure encrypted satellite call to headquarters. Tony picked up with Stan and Tom also present on the line.

"Janusz, what did you find out from Johan?"

"Johan was unable to communicate when we met last night."

"Why the hell not?"

"His tongue had been cut out by the IRGC before my arrival. Even better, they had placed explosives in his house primed to go off as I stood in the dining room."

"How did they know you were coming?"

"Our activities have been compromised. Most likely, Massoud has had a change of heart or has set us up from the beginning. We need another avenue to gain clarity on the Buraq Project."

"What do you want to do about this?"

"I need to think. In the meantime, I'm going to Melbourne for a few days to attend to personal business."

Having cheated death and lost an associate, Janusz was mentally exhausted. He called Jennifer and asked her to meet him in Melbourne. It was essential to have a few days with her in the middle of all this madness.

24. IRGC JOINT STAFF HEADQUARTERS, EASTERN TEHRAN, IRAN

October 30

Hassan Hashemi sat outside Colonel Ramazani's office. He had been waiting for over thirty minutes past his appointment with the colonel, but he didn't mind. Each time he was called to meet with the boss at headquarters, it was to discuss a "special project." He lost track of time while reading about the soft threats to the regime in Sobhe-Sadegh, a weekly newspaper published by the political office of the supreme leader's representative to the IRGC. He was so preoccupied with the article he didn't notice Colonel Ramazani standing over his shoulder. The colonel gently tapped his arm.

"Sorry, sir, this article highlights a few questions I need to ask our prisoners. I didn't notice you standing there."

"This is why I admire you, Hassan. You're always focused on protecting our revolution."

"Most kind of you, sir."

"Come inside my office. I've got another special project for you." As Hassan settled into the chair, Colonel Ramazani shuffled a few papers on his desk. Hassan's popularity with the IRGC high command had come as a surprise. He had always been a skilled interrogator. Word had spread quickly about his effectiveness at Evin prison. Hassan had been initially hired by the rival MOIS to work in section 209 at Evin prison. He eventually became the chief interrogator for the MOIS with a stellar reputation for extracting confessions out of the most obstinate inmates.

His ingenuity in devising painful punishments for enemies of the regime was legendary. It must have been quite a blow to the MOIS to have him resign. The IRGC-IO had offered him a generous bonus plan for hard-to-come-by confessions. It was annoying how many regime officials forgot that hard work required adequate compensation. Hassan was now in charge of a new ward in Evin, section 2A, administered by the IRGC-IO.

"Hassan, the reason I called you here today—" Before he finished his sentence, the Colonel was interrupted by a phone call.

"Yes. I'm in the middle of something," Colonel Ramazani replied.

"Sir, I'm afraid I have some bad news. Our man got away." The voice on the other end of the line was screaming for some reason.

"What do you mean he got away?"

"I mean our trap didn't work."

"Are you sure?"

"He ran out of the house after the explosion."

"Well, why the fuck didn't you go back to finish the job?"

"We couldn't exactly risk getting caught by the Icelandic authorities. You were the one who said, 'no matter what happens, do not get caught dead or alive.'"

"Where are you now?"

"We're still in Iceland."

"Then don't waste any more time talking to me. Get the hell out of there!"

Colonel Ramazani was silent before returning to Hassan. "Okay, where was I? Yes, I called you here today because I want you to work on a special guest in section 2A. His name is Ismail Safavi. My men have arrested him on suspicion of membership in the Hojjatieh Society." Colonel Ramazani suddenly drifted off once more. It took a moment before he was able to finish his thought.

"Ismail is not being very cooperative with my men. I need

you to—how should I put it—loosen his tongue. I must warn you, he's quite adamant that he has nothing to say."

"Not to worry, sir. I assure you that even the most determined man will crack with the use of proper methods."

"Very well, a driver is waiting for us outside. He'll take us to Evin where Ismail is currently detained. I'd like to stay in the background as you work on him."

"I must warn you, sir, we may not be able to break him right away. It may take several days before he opens up."

"No problem. I'll observe as you start the process. You can continue your work after I leave. But you must call me as soon as he begins to talk." Colonel Ramazani grabbed his jacket. Ten minutes later, they were on Yasini Highway, heading north toward Evin.

25. EVIN PRISON, NORTHERN TEHRAN, IRAN

October 30

Evin prison sat at the foot of the Alborz Mountains in the northeast corner of Tehran. To the north and east, it was surrounded by a barren landscape with high concrete walls, topped with barbed wire. The prison was built during the reign of the Shah. It had been administered by the Shah's internal security service, SAVAK. No one had ever escaped from this prison, which was why the Islamic authorities had adopted it. Currently, several security organizations jointly operated the various wings of Evin. Overcrowding was a perennial problem, although multiple cells operated by both the IRGC and MOIS were reserved for solitary confinement. The protocol was so strict that none of the inmates could even recognize the hallway outside of their cells. Prisoners were blindfolded whenever they were moved around or taken to interrogation.

Colonel Ramazani accompanied Hassan as they took the elevator several levels below ground to a special interrogation room with no natural lights. The room was pitch black, except for a sixty-watt bulb attached to the ceiling with copper wire. Two chairs had been placed underneath the light along with a table, on top of which sat several instruments. Along the wall, outside the view of those sitting under the light, a number of chairs had been placed for observers. Colonel Ramazani sat in one of those chairs, hidden by darkness, while Hassan made himself comfortable. Five minutes later, two IRGC guards walked in slowly while guiding the blindfolded Ismail Safavi. The prisoner was seated on the chair in front of Hassan. The master interrogator immediately removed the cover from his eyes. Hassan preferred to stare into a man's eyes during an interrogation.

"Ismail, you've been brought here because you haven't cooperated with my colleagues. If you play ball, I promise to get you out of here as soon as possible. If you refuse, I guarantee that everything that's happened to you thus far will feel like a pleasant stroll in the park."

Ismail stared into Hassan's eyes without saying a word. It was going to be a long afternoon.

"Who is the top man in the Hojjatieh?" There was silence. Hassan waited another minute. "Ismail, who is the leader of the Hojjatieh?"

"What is the Hojjatieh?" came the reply. The next sound to fill the room was a thunderous clap. Ismail was thrown out of his seat by the blow.

"Perhaps the first question was too hard. How many individuals are members of the Hojjatieh?"

Silence once again.

Hassan punched the prisoner in the face, causing his chair to fall back toward the ground. For the next thirty minutes, the interrogation room was filled by the sounds of slaps and punches. The prisoner did not break. It seemed that they would not get anything useful out of this inmate—at least not today.

As Hassan administered the next round of blows, Colonel Ramazani quietly got up and walked out of the room. Based on the number of reports filed by his men, the Hojjatieh was now the top threat to the regime. They needed more suspects. Colonel Ramazani was confident that Hassan would help the IRGC get to the bottom of the Hojjatieh's activities. One way or the other, they would eventually get what they needed from that despicable Ismail Safavi.

26. QANTAS AIR FLIGHT, ABOVE THE SOUTH PACIFIC OCEAN

November 01

The captain of the Qantas Air Airbus 380 had just announced they would be landing in Melbourne sooner than expected. Jennifer finished her salmon dinner with champagne in the first-class cabin. She miraculously got some time off to visit Janusz despite a last minute request. She had already watched two full-length movies on the sixteen-hour flight from Los Angeles, the last leg of her journey from Washington. She wondered if it was wise to confront Janusz about his gambling. She preferred to let him deal with the issue on his own, but the longer she waited, the worse he could get. It was the hardest conversation she had ever prepared for. How could she live with herself if she didn't try? Janusz was waiting for her when she exited customs. She jumped into his arms as soon as they met. He immediately drove back to the apartment on Collins Street.

A few minutes later, they were taking the elevator to his condominium. Janusz suddenly spoke, "Jennifer, I know the past few months haven't been easy for you. I promise things will be different when—" As the elevator doors opened on the thirty-third floor, she stood there waiting for him to finish his sentence. "Come on, we can't hang out in the elevator all day."

"Uff-da, just finish your sentence!"

He grabbed her arm, dragging her into the apartment. Once inside, he put her bags down and turned. She was staring at him by the doorway.

"You betcha things will be different. For one, I don't plan on being with a man who destroys himself. If you keep this up, you're going to wake up having lost everything, including me." She paused for a breath, but the words rushed out of her. "You should know that your parents told me everything, including what happened to your brother. You need to help yourself before I can help you. It was one thing to start gambling to cope with the loss of Ben. You did what you had to do. But that's in the past, and it's time to move on. You have to admit you have a problem before you can get better."

Janusz looked at her for a few seconds. "I'm glad you spoke with my parents. I asked you here so we could have a few days just to ourselves. I'll address this issue with you later, but right now, let's please not think about anything else except you and me."

She considered his proposal and walked over to hug him. They spent the rest of the day in each other's embrace.

When the sun set, Jennifer fell asleep on Janusz's chest until the next morning. She woke up to a delightful aroma. The table had already been set in the dining room. Janusz was making her favorite breakfast: Belgian waffles topped with fresh strawberry jam and whipped cream. At the center of the table was a vase filled with a dozen flowers. Red rose petals and lavender stems were spread between the dishes on the table.

"When did you have time to do all this?"

"When you were asleep. I was restless, so I decided to do something useful."

"Well, I'm glad you've had time to improve your culinary skills."

"I have a special day planned for us. You're going to need your energy."

"So tell me, what's inspired your interest in cooking? You rarely make breakfast back home."

"I had to adapt to the bachelor's life while you weren't around."

"Really? You never told me exactly why they kept you here for so long?"

"It was all part of Tony's plan to get us Australian citizenship. He explained we could travel to more places as Aussies. I'm sorry I haven't been more available."

Jennifer nodded in acknowledgment. They spent the time enjoying each other's company. He took her to a nearby park where they walked through the trails during the afternoon. They had dinner at an upscale Italian restaurant. The next three days were full of adventure. They went to museums, rode bikes, and did some sailing.

On the last morning, Janusz dropped her off at the airport. She wondered if she would ever see him again.

Several hours later, Janusz set up a secure Video Teleconference (VTC) with Headquarters. All members of the Australian team were present along with the principals back home.

"Gentlemen, during the flight back from Iceland, I remembered recruiting a high-level source in the IRGC while I was on assignment with the CIA. Unfortunately, the Agency had terminated him in the mistaken belief that he wasn't responsive to tasking. I pushed back, trying to explain that the source's position in the IRGC Joint Staff was so sensitive that he could not afford to perform any trick that management at Langley requested. They wouldn't listen and ordered me to let him go. That, by the way, was the incident that prompted me to resign."

"What are you getting at?" Tony said.

"I maintained contact with him after I left the Agency. The last time we spoke, he was still under the impression that I'm his CIA contact."

"What's this man's role?"

"He's a Brigadier General in the IRGC's Joint Staff. He is also the deputy to the IRGC Commander with insight into all their covert weapons programs."

"A Brigadier General? How did the Agency let that one get away?"

"Tony, do you really want me to answer that question?"

"Forget I asked. Tell me, how can you be sure he is still willing to work with us?" Tony said.

"I'm not sure. As a matter of fact, I never met with him in Tehran. All our meetings took place when he went on vacation with his family to Turkey." Janusz remembered driving around Istanbul while he debriefed the General. He would then drop him off near a museum before riding off.

"Won't he be frightened to meet in Tehran?"

"Probably. We're running out of time with no leads. Got a better idea?"

"Very well. Do you want to take anyone with you?" Tony said.

"It's best if I went in alone on this one. I don't want to risk other lives on a gamble."

The meeting rooms fell silent. No one from the Unit had traveled to Iran up to that point.

"Teresa will help you set up your flight itinerary while we create your cover persona. Good luck," Tony said.

Teresa Jenkins was an attractive Australian woman in her mid-thirties, in charge of Human Resources for Oceana. She had tried to seduce Janusz not long ago, but he had rebuffed her advances. Perhaps it was another sign that he was truly in love with Jennifer.

27. MELBOURNE AIRPORT, AUSTRALIA

November 08

At half-past nine in the evening, the Emirates Air flight attendant made the boarding call for the Boeing 777-300 flight to Dubai. Janusz would then catch a connecting flight scheduled to arrive in Tehran at nine-thirty in the morning. As he stood up to get in line to board, he was overcome by an unfamiliar sensation. He finally acknowledged to himself that he was nervous. It was a good feeling; it kept a man on his toes. He had completed many missions for his beloved America. The difference this time was that he had ancestral roots in his destination.

There was no denying the fact that, despite his hatred for the current regime, he had Persian blood flowing through his veins. Iran was where Cyrus the Great had decreed a universal declaration of human rights over two thousand five hundred years ago. It was a country whose people had given to the world Polo, backgammon, and chess. Janusz presented his boarding pass to the flight attendant. She flirted with her eyes. "Have a wonderful trip, Mr. Phillips."

Several other men in business suits walked to the first-class cabin in front of him. It was a bit of a letdown after flying in the Gulfstream. He had grown accustomed to the G650, but it was out of the question for the purposes of this mission. Besides, the first-class cabin of Emirates Air was the next best thing to a private jet. Janusz hung his coat on the rack in his cabin, which had its own door and a minibar. His seat converted to a comfortable full flatbed. He had brought some reading material, including a few magazines and brochures from several Iranian companies. Oceana was supposedly considering investing in those companies as part of his cover story. A gorgeous Chinese stewardess stood over his shoulder.

"Can I get you anything, sir?"

This was perhaps the best feature of Emirates Air. The airline was a virtual United Nations of beautiful women from around the world. The Arabs who ran the airline wouldn't have it any other way.

"A glass of red wine, please."

As the flight attendant walked away, his thoughts immediately drifted to washing her naked body in the shower. He refocused by reviewing his cover story for the upcoming mission. One small slip and this would be his last assignment on earth. He had not even said goodbye to his parents.

"Here you are, sir." The flight attendant handed him a glass of wine. "Please fasten your seat belt; we're about to take off."

Janusz sipped his wine while reviewing his notes. He was Ian Phillips, a partner at an Australian private equity firm, Oceana. His company was interested in acquiring a stake in several Iranian mining entities trading on the Tehran Stock Exchange. The Iranians had recently courted foreign investors to enter into partnership agreements. They needed an infusion of foreign capital as well as technology. It was the perfect opportunity for Oceana. Janusz was familiar with the Iranian equities market, given his research on the acquisition of Rostami Partners.

Ayatollah Mashhadi had recently decided to expand his personal wealth by privatizing a segment of the Iranian economy. As always, the IRGC benefited from his largesse. In the early days of the revolution, the Iranian government had nationalized all major industrial firms. The recent consolidation of power by Ayatollah Mashhadi and the IRGC allowed most valuable state assets to be privatized by a handful of insiders with ties to the supreme leader. Ayatollah Mashhadi had suddenly declared that investment in the stock market was a virtuous activity in order to drive up the share prices in these newly privatized companies. This proclamation had led to the expansion of the financial industry through the creation of new investment funds bringing billions of dollars into the Tehran Stock Exchange.

Janusz had appointments to meet several managers from these firms. A letter sent on his behalf from the First Australia Bank indicated that Ian Phillips had access to a credit line of one hundred million dollars. Oceana had also declared its intention to invest at least fifty million dollars in Iran. The bank letter was meant to coax the Iranians into working to win his favor. Janusz flipped through a brochure for Pars Aluminum. The company, headquartered in Isfahan, was traded on the Tehran Stock Exchange valued at four billion dollars. Curiously, forty percent of Pars Aluminum's shares were owned by a holding company managed on behalf of Ayatollah Mashhadi. Another holding company with ties to the IRGC held forty-five percent of the shares. Ordinary Iranian investors owned only fifteen percent of Pars Aluminum. Most other public companies on the Tehran Stock Exchange had a similar ownership structure.

Another scheme allowed Ayatollah Mashhadi, using proceeds from the seized assets of Iranian expats living abroad, to become rich. A foundation called "The Charity for Fulfilling the Imam's Wishes" invested a portion of the proceeds from the property seizures into buying shares of publicly traded companies. The combined value of the investments controlled by Ayatollah Mashhadi and his appointees was estimated at over one hundred billion dollars. If accurate, the figure meant that the Iranian supreme leader was easily one of the richest men in the world. It was unfortunate that Forbes magazine was not familiar with asset valuation in a country like Iran.

As the engines roared, Janusz tightened his seatbelt while the landscape raced by outside his window. Once airborne, the lights from downtown Melbourne's high-rises sparkled like jewels. He was immediately transported to his high school days at Woodbury Forest in Virginia. He spent four years at that boarding school not far from Montpelier, Virginia, where his favorite president, James Madison, had lived. He had been a star wrestler in those days.

It was at Woodbury Forest where a classmate, John Donavan, first sparked his curiosity about international affairs. Years later, he learned that John's father had worked for the CIA. John's family had a large estate near Middleburg where they would throw parties to which Janusz was invited. John Senior told interesting stories about travels to faraway locations such as Kampala, Katmandu, Colombo, and Islamabad.

It was a story about US efforts to end communism in Poland that made him curious about the CIA. Janusz was now in a position to help shape events in another country. Unlike Mr. Donovan, Janusz was no longer bound to a large government bureaucracy, allowing him to exercise more personal initiative than John Donavan Sr. could have ever imagined. As he pondered what Mr. Donavan would say about the Unit's unique mission, Janusz fell asleep.

He woke seven hours later as the pilot announced the final preparations for landing. His pillow was completely wet with drool. After a six-hour stopover in Dubai, he boarded the plane to Tehran. He drifted off into thoughts about Jennifer and whether he would ever see her again. The next sounds were the pilot's announcement. "Ladies and gentlemen, welcome to Tehran where the local time is 9:30 a.m."

Damn, when did the wheels touch the ground? They were now taxiing on the runway. Outside the window, Imam Khomeini International Airport didn't seem that different from any other airport. That was the strange thing about airports. They were all the same no matter where you went.

He grabbed his bag while walking off the plane with the rest of the group. They walked through a series of corridors where bearded security officers kept a vigilant eye on the new arrivals at several intervals along the way. He finally arrived at the main security kiosk where he presented his passport to the official behind the glass. To his surprise, it was a woman. She appeared no older than thirty-five, and she wore very little makeup. Her black headscarf covered her face ever so tightly, not allowing even a single strand of hair to escape. She flipped through the pages of his passport in search of something. Perhaps she was looking for an entry or exit stamp of the State of Israel.

"What's the purpose of your visit to the Islamic Republic, Mr. Phillips?"

"Business. I'm considering investing in Iranian companies."

"How long are you staying?"

"Three weeks, maybe longer, depending on how long it takes to arrange meetings with various company representatives."

She maintained a scowl during their conversation. It was as though she was getting ready to perform an execution. Most Westerners generally tried to appear friendly, at least in public, but not her. "Do you plan on doing any sightseeing while in Iran?"

"Not unless my local associates take me to their facilities outside of Tehran."

"Can you provide the name for any company you're meeting with?"

"Pars Aluminum. They've done very well over the past few years."

The woman was suddenly more at ease. "What a coincidence! My uncle is a plant manager at one of their facilities here in Tehran."

It was hard to imagine that of all the companies in Iran where her uncle could've worked, it had to be the one he had chosen as a backstop for his visit here.

"Good luck, Mr. Phillips. Enjoy your stay."

She proceeded to pound his passport with the entry stamp of the Islamic Republic of Iran.

It was time to walk through the maze once again. This

time it was customs that opened his bags to ruffle through his clothes in search of contraband, perhaps alcohol. The regime assumed Westerners could not live without getting drunk, even for a few days. The customs agent, an IRGC officer, asked Janusz a set of questions similar to the ones he had just answered. Finally, after twenty minutes, he was outside the main terminal in search of a taxi. It was not as bad as he had expected, but the most dangerous part of traveling to Iran would be on the way out.

To her chagrin, an Iranian-American had discovered that fact a few years earlier when she tried to go home after visiting her ailing father. The entry process had been as pleasant as the previous times she had visited. On the way out, however, her passport had been confiscated by the IRGC-IO. She was detained for several months on the charge that she was a CIA spy. She was finally released after the president of the United States had personally requested she be allowed to leave. Janusz would not be able to rely on similar favors.

28. THE HOTEL ESPINAS, TEHRAN, IRAN

November 09

The taxi dropped him off at his temporary residence in Tehran. The Hotel Espinas was among the more upscale establishments in the sprawling metropolis of fourteen million. The lobby was quite impressive. Coffered ceiling supported by white columns adorned the entire space. Granite floors were covered with intricate Persian rugs. Two large stone statues, a man and a woman, resembling works from the Parthian Empire were placed on either side of the walkway leading to the front desk. A picture of Ayatollah Semnani had been placed on the top of the column to the right of the front desk while a picture of Ayatollah Mashhadi covered the top of the column to the left. These were reminders of the ultimate authority in the country. The receptionist was an attractive Iranian woman with radiant light skin. Although her hair was covered as required by law, she had an infectious smile with beautiful green eyes. It took Janusz several seconds to remember why he was standing there as he gazed at her.

"Good morning. I'm Ian Phillips. I'd like to check-in."

"Good morning, Mr. Phillips! My name is Pega. I'll be happy to assist you. Passport, please!"

Janusz placed the passport on the counter. She skimmed through it and typed his information into the computer. "Here you go, Mr. Phillips. Your room is all set. Give us a call if you need anything."

Under different circumstances, he would have asked for her number, but that was definitely out of the question now. He thanked her in Persian, "*Kheili Mamnoun*." Janusz took the elevators to the fifth floor where his room was located. Inside, the accommodations were satisfactory. The interior decorations matched his own classic style, making him feel strangely at home. He placed his bags in the closet before walking over to the glass-top desk where he placed his briefcase. Using the hotel phone, he contacted Hessam Jafaari, the CEO of Pars Aluminum, to arrange a meeting the next day. For anyone listening in, it was proof he had legitimate business in Iran. With that out of the way, Janusz took an ordinary-looking laptop out of his briefcase. He drafted an email asking to meet with Brigadier General Reza Zanjani of the IRGC Joint Staff. General Zanjani was also the highest-ranking official ever recruited by the CIA due to his efforts. Janusz had reestablished contact after joining the Unit.

The laptop had been configured with custom stenographic software. The program allowed for embedding secret messages within a seemingly innocuous picture file. This was one of the many techniques, referred to as COVCOM or covert communications, at the CIA. Intelligence services around the world used this type of software for secret communications with their assets. It was the preferred method to evade counter-espionage surveillance by hostile security services. Janusz used the hotel Wi-Fi signal to send the message after the encryption software had done its work. The laptop was also configured for silent keystrokes. It was used to evade listening devices that translated keystrokes into the corresponding letter on a computer. A thin filter that prevented hidden cameras from recording the screen display covered the laptop's monitor.

The email content was similar to a routine correspondence between General Zanjani and his son, Majid, at the University of Shiraz. Janusz had previously used this technique for communicating with the General. It had remained their primary communication method. The encrypted message read:

Just arrived in Tehran, need to meet with you as soon as possible. I'm authorized to pay you a million dollars in exchange for the extra risk you're being asked to take for a Tehran meeting. If face-to-face meeting is not possible, we can correspond through our alternate email arrangement.

29. MALARD MISSILE RESEARCH FACILITY, WESTERN TEHRAN, IRAN

November 09

The director drank his third cup of black tea. It was impossible to stay awake. He had spent the previous evening in the lab experimenting with a new formula for the Buraq missile. The clock was ticking, and he had little to show. Colonel Ramazani's men had already spoken to Massoud in Malaysia. They had also killed a member of the Hojjatieh. The word spread quickly that Ismail Safavi had died under a brutal interrogation at Evin. The director was convinced that their only chance for success was to purchase the required fuel from abroad. His eyelids were halfway closed when a ringing phone startled him.

"Good morning, Ostad! I've found a new potential supplier for the program in Singapore. A company called Canton Trading. I've made arrangements for a meeting later today."

"Excellent, Massoud. May Allah bless you with eternal health! Have there been any more visits from Colonel Ramazani's men?"

"No, but I suspect we've not heard the last from them."

"We can't afford to worry about that now. Try to stay out of their way and keep me updated on new developments."

"Will do."

"*Ya Abolfazl,* we're excited about your return. May Allah keep you safe!"

The call changed the director's mood. For the first time in

months, he was optimistic. He was about to use the bathroom when someone entered his office without knocking.

"Ostad, you should come to the composites lab at once. There is something I want to share with you."

Curse that damn Yazid! Can't a man take a piss without being disturbed around here?

It was Mohammad Assadolahi, the program manager in the composites division. His team had been working around the clock to create carbon composite motors, nozzles, and frames for the Buraq. The completed missile had to withstand the extreme heat of combustion in its motor, and the nozzle had to tolerate high exhaust temperatures without erosion. Since carbon composites were on average about thirty percent lighter than the metals they had been using thus far, the Buraq could travel farther using the same amount of fuel.

Perhaps it was going to be a good day after all. He turned to Assadolahi.

"Please go back to the lab and wait for me there. I need to take care of a minor detail."

With Assadolahi out of his hair, the director walked to his private bathroom and relieved himself in peace. A few minutes later, he made his way over to hangar number 4. The engineers of the composites team were huddled together when he arrived. As he approached, he was greeted by shouts of *"Zende bad Hossein, Marg bar Yazid!"* *Long live Hossein, death to Yazid!* The team members approached one-by-one to shake his hand. The director kept repeating the phrase, *"Khaste Nabashid,"* wishing them *boundless energy.*

He finally quizzed Assadolahi, whispering into his ear, "What's the cause of all this enthusiasm?"

"Ostad, we wanted to surprise you. We've made a breakthrough that'll allow the Buraq to reach its maximum intended range."

"Ya Abolfazl, please continue."

"We've had success with composite motor casings and nozzles."

Composites were manufactured by joining two or more materials with significantly different physical and chemical properties. When combined, the materials produced a substance with characteristics different from those of its individual components. Specifically, carbon composites combined carbon with plastic, fiberglass, graphite, or even aluminum. These composites were much lighter than non-composite metals such as steel, aluminum, or titanium, traditionally used for the construction of missile components.

"Our tests with carbon-carbon composites yielded both a high-heat and a high-impact resistant material. We then built several experimental nozzles and motor casings exclusively of the same material. Once the prototypes were ready, we studied the composites in our test chamber to measure resistance to thermal shock." Assadolahi said.

The director was so tired it took him a few minutes to remember the concepts from materials engineering. Thermal shock occurs when rapidly changing temperatures cause different parts of an object to expand at different increments. This differential expansion or contraction of the material causes both strain and stress. At some point, the stress can exceed the tensile strength of the material, causing a crack to form. This crack can ultimately propagate throughout the material, causing structural failure. Thermal shock testing exposes the experimental carbon-carbon composite to alternating high/low temperatures to accelerate the failures that could arise from thermal shock during normal use.

"Ostad, I'll just take a minute to describe our experiments. Our vertical dual-zone test chamber contains both hot and cold zones that can be controlled independently. A dual compartment product carrier simultaneously moves our composite material between the hot and cold zones."

Assadolahi glanced at his boss for feedback. The director grinned, signaling his willingness to hear more.

"To measure the stress of exposure in the thermal shock test chamber, we attached several strain gauges on our composite material. Our gauge, resembling a Band-Aid, is attached to the composite material with an adhesive. The variations in temperature inside the chamber cause the composite to change in size due to thermal expansion. These changes are detected as a strain by the gauge. Once the test results proved our team had successfully created a composite resistant to thermal shock, we began assembling motor casings and nozzles using the new material." Assadolahi said while guiding the director around the equipment.

"Before I continue, I'd like to add that we've also purchased two German Coordinate Measuring Machines (CMM) to accurately measure the various components produced here at the lab. This allows us to implement the latest quality control measures used by Westerners to ensure the reliability of our manufactured products." Assadolahi said.

"I hope you kept an eye on costs."

"Of course. As a matter of fact, the CMMs are great because they aid in product development, manufacturing, and assembly. They allow us to compare various parts against design drawings during the inspection. With the aid of the CMMs, we've assembled several motor casings that were immediately subjected to hydrostatic tests to measure the amount of pressure that the motor can handle along with possible cracks. Since an undetected crack as small as one thirty-second of an inch can cause a disastrous failure, we tested our motors above normal operating pressure. This allows the prompt detection of serious defects. During hydrostatic testing, the combustion chamber is filled with a nearly incompressible liquid, such as water, examining for leaks or permanent changes in shape. A fluorescent dye is added to the water to make leaks easier to detect. After several rounds of tests, we've not detected a single crack or change in shape using our proprietary composite carbon material." Assadolahi said before turning to the chief composites technician, "Fariborz, please remove the cover."

Fariborz walked over to a control panel that manipulated a large mechanical arm. After he pushed a button, the mechanical arm removed the cloth cover that concealed a three-meter-diameter missile motor made entirely of a carbon-carbon composite material. The composite motor resembled a large shiny black drum on the outside. Fariborz pushed another button, which removed the cover from a motor nozzle also made completely from a carbon-carbon composite.

"Ostad, I present you with our completed missile motors and nozzles made entirely of the most advanced carbon composite materials. They're resistant to both thermal shock and high-impact strain. We believe even the Americans have not been able to manufacture composites with these characteristics."

The director walked over to Assadolahi, placing a firm kiss squarely on his lips. The rest of the men slapped each other on the back. The director spoke once more, this time more firmly, as if issuing a command.

"Listen to me carefully, Assadolahi. You must immediately commence the production of twelve Buraq missiles using the new carbon composites you've produced here. The hour of Imam Mahdi's arrival is at hand."

30. LAVIZAN, NORTH EASTERN TEHRAN, IRAN

November 09

G eneral Zanjani had been home for less than an hour when he walked over to his private study in the luxury apartment he shared with his wife. He sat behind a desktop computer, bought at a substantial discount from the IRGC social services division. There was one new email in the account he used to communicate with the American. He opened the message, which contained an attachment. It was a picture of his son, Majid, at the university.

When the stenographic software deciphered the message within the picture, he was surprised to find out that his CIA contact was in Tehran. The one million dollars being offered for meeting locally more than made up for the extra risk he was being asked to take. The money would allow the general to take his family out of the country if need be. He decided to accept the risky request for a Tehran meeting. Similar to his high-ranking colleagues in the IRGC, General Zanjani had access to an apartment purchased under the name of his mistress. He sent his reply using a separate encrypted file.

Please come to 11 Shian Street, apartment number eight, tomorrow night at 7:00 p.m. You can take the Tehran metro line number 3 to the Hossein Abad Square station. From there, you will walk the rest of the way. Knock four times and wait until I open the door.

General Zanjani then uploaded a picture of himself standing next to his wife in the park. He used the stenographic software previously provided by his contact to embed his message before hitting send. He sent the message while wondering why the CIA had come to Iran to visit him personally. Could it be that they wanted to kill him? Why would they do that? He had provided them with valuable information about the IRGC for years. Perhaps they were after someone else. There was only one way to find out.

General Zanjani had once been a loyal member of the IRGC. He had moved up the chain of command through hard work. He was from a devout family that supported the revolution from the beginning. As he climbed the ladder of success, he helped himself to some side benefits of membership in the IRGC. This arrangement meant access to low-interest loans for personal investment and gain. General Zanjani and a few others had used their connections to borrow the equivalent of five million dollars for the purchase of an import-export business. When a periodic internal investigation led to only his arrest, he resented being singled out for punishment.

Although he had not been relieved of command, General Zanjani had to pay back the borrowed principal in addition to an exorbitant interest rate. Several other generals, arrested in the same operation, had been able to escape a similar fate due to their connections with high-ranking officials. The whole thing had left a bad taste in his mouth. To add insult to injury, he had been temporarily demoted to colonel for a period of a year. The incident had pushed him toward the Americans. He had first approached the American Embassy in Ankara while on a vacation with his family. That's where he'd met a man named John King.

General Zanjani had given the Americans access to the most sensitive secrets of the IRGC Joint Staff. His position as an assistant to the IRGC Commander, General Mohsen Jafarzadeh, had provided insight into every compartmented program run by the IRGC, including the Iranian nuclear weapons program.

The Americans had wanted to cut him loose when he refused to take their silly polygraph test. However, John King had come to his rescue. Now he was here to give him a million dollars. What did he want in return?

31. PARCHIN ARMAMENTS COMPLEX, SOUTH EASTERN TEHRAN, IRAN

November 09

Pavel Yevchenko was reviewing the latest implosion test results at lab number 8 of the Parchin Complex. The latest tests had all been successful. He was confident his design for the six hundred kilogram, fifty-kiloton-yield warhead, was optimal for the Buraq missile.

Pavel had spent his childhood in the Soviet city of Leningrad, which later reverted back to its original name of St. Petersburg. The fifty-five-year-old scientist had been living in Iran for the past five years.

This morning, Pavel was poring over the blueprints for warhead number P5000 with Iranian engineers, satisfied the designs were ready to be submitted to the Defense Industries Organization for serial production. The IRGC had finally delivered the twelve hundred kilograms of ninety percent highly-enriched uranium (HEU) from its secret uranium conversion/enrichment facilities, buried deep inside a mountain near the Iranian city of Shiraz. The guards had developed this clandestine infrastructure for converting uranium ore into yellowcake, which was subsequently converted into the UF6 feedstock for the undeclared cascade of over ten thousand centrifuges. From there, the UF6 was enriched all the way to ninety percent.

A shell company with no direct ties to Iran secretly mined some of the uranium ore in Africa. The rest had been mined in Iran undeclared to the international community.

Pavel's design would allow the Defense Industries Organization to build twelve warheads using the twelve hundred kilograms of HEU delivered to several underground factories. He had been promised a two hundred fifty thousand dollar bonus for his efforts to deliver the warheads ahead of schedule. For this reason, he had spent the last four weeks sleeping in the lab at Parchin.

The realization that his work with the clerical regime made him a target of assassination by a variety of intelligence services had not been a deterrent. The risk was worth the alternative. For close to a decade after the end of the Cold War, he could not find gainful employment in Russia after his termination from the weapons research division of the Russian Ministry of Defense. It was a humiliating experience for someone with a PhD in nuclear physics from the Moscow Institute of Physics and Technology. In Iran, he was in charge of his own destiny once again. More importantly, he was engaged in intellectually stimulating work. The Iranians treated him with greater respect than did his own comrades. To top it all off, he was provided with luxuries that Russian nuclear scientists could only dream of. The Iranians had built him a custom-designed mansion in the upscale Tehran neighborhood of *Shahrak-e Gharb* with an indoor swimming pool. In addition to his considerable salary, he was provided with a security detail during his travels around the country. His life in Iran was going well despite the cultural differences. What the Iranians chose to do with their weapons was none of his business. Was it any worse than the thousands of nuclear warheads his fellow Russian scientists had designed for the Kremlin?

Today was a special day at the lab. Pavel had a scheduled meeting with a guest. President Azari was coming to learn about the progress of the nuclear warheads, and Pavel didn't want to disappoint him. He had met with President Azari on at least seven separate occasions over the past six months. On at least two of those occasions, the President had screamed at Pavel in Farsi when told about a delay in the program. And on one of those occasions, President Azari had thrown a pen at him. Pavel had ducked just in time. Fortunately, he had only good news to deliver today. He was about to bite into an apple when the office phone rang. It was his personal assistant.

"What is it, Maryam? I'm busy."

"Just thought you'd like to know that President Azari, Admiral Abbasi, and General Jafarzadeh have arrived."

"Please escort them to the conference room."

Pavel walked toward the conference room as quickly as he could to arrive before the visiting delegation. He was setting up the slide presentation when they entered through the door.

"Good morning, gentlemen. I've been looking forward to this meeting," Pavel said.

The IRGC was in charge of Iran's nuclear weapons program, and it was not unusual for the Commander of the Guards and the Defense Minister, both IRGC officers, to check on the progress in person. President Azari had established a precedent early in his administration for taking an active interest in military affairs.

"Pavel, I trust you've got good news for us?" President Azari said.

"I do indeed, sir. Over the past month, we've conducted several computer simulations of the nuclear warhead design I've developed for the Defense Industries Organization. I'm happy to report that all simulation tests have been successful. Our final blueprint is ready. We can move forward with production immediately."

"Excellent," President Azari said.

"I've prepared a slide show detailing our accomplishments. We can begin if someone will turn off the lights."

"That won't be necessary, Pavel. Send copies of your presentation to my assistant. I'll review them in my office. I must run to another meeting," President Azari said as he walked out the door.

32. REZA ZANJANI'S APARTMENT, LAVIZAN, NORTH EASTERN TEHRAN, IRAN

November 09

T he number 3 train to Hossein Abad Square was full of passengers returning home from work. It was ten past six, and the evening rush hour was in full swing. Janusz was wearing a disguise. Ed Wright from the Unit, a wizard with disguises, had given him a makeup bag to help him blend in. Ed had also provided Iranian identification if Janusz was to be stopped by the authorities for any reason.

When he got off the train, Janusz was impressed by the cleanliness of the Hossein Abad Square Metro station. The walls were adorned with rows of artwork. Shiny yellow chairs in mint condition were available throughout the platform. There were no mechanical delays with any of the trains, and the escalators were all in working order. It was definitely a better-maintained system than the one operated by the Washington Metropolitan Transit Authority back home. Perhaps the officials of D.C. metro needed to visit Tehran for a lesson on how to run an urban metro system. Once at street level, he walked over to General Zanjani's apartment, keeping an eye out for possible surveillance.

He was finally in the land of his ancestors. Janusz had dreamt of this day since he was a child but had not anticipated the circumstances. In contrast to the present leadership, Cyrus the Great had championed human rights for all citizens in his empire over twenty-five centuries earlier. Modern Iranians, however, could be sentenced to death for speaking out against their government. This was a country where stoning adulterers was still practiced. It was also a country where individuals convicted of cutting off the ear or gouging out the eye of a victim could expect the exact same treatment from the courts. Who could forget the political opponents locked up for years without charge for criticizing the regime? It made his blood boil that the leaders of this country had the audacity to claim that their economic woes were the result of international sanctions. Apparently, they had forgotten their neglect of economic planning.

Then there was the business with his brother. The leaders of Iran were ultimately responsible for approving the bombing in Rome that had killed Ben. Eliminating Hamid Ajami had only dealt with the problem of the triggerman. Hamid's masters in Tehran had not yet received their just reward. Janusz had to succeed for all these reasons, and above all, to settle the account of Benjamin Soltani.

He rang the bell in front of the building at 7:05 p.m. The door opened. Janusz went upstairs and knocked four times as they had agreed.

"*Salam*, please come in," General Zanjani said in Farsi. "I like your disguise. You look Iranian."

"Thank you."

"What brings you to Tehran? You're taking a great risk."

General Zanjani's uneasiness was palpable. Janusz reached into his pocket to remove a small pouch that he tossed on a nearby table. "Before I forget, here is the million dollars I promised. I hope you won't mind taking payment in stones. These diamonds have an estimated value closer to one point two million. They'll be easier for you to take out of the country."

General Zanjani already had a house in Canada where he could run to in an emergency, provided he could leave the country in one piece.

"Let's get down to business. The longer I'm here, the more

likely we're both dead by tomorrow. What do you know about the IRGC's Buraq missile program? Why is the IRGC now developing missiles?"

General Zanjani took a few puffs of his cigarette, gazing around the room before he answered the question. He seemed calmer after Janusz revealed what he was after.

"I know the supreme leader only trusts the IRGC for our most sensitive military projects. The answer to the second part of your question is the reason for my heartache. I hope you'll have enough time to stop what's coming."

Janusz's stomach sank; his worries about the Buraq program were justified.

"What I'm about to tell you is something I suspect even the supreme leader is not aware of." General Zanjani took another puff from his cigarette. "Ten years ago, Ayatollah Mashhadi concluded that the only way to ensure the survival of his regime was to develop a nuclear weapon. Naturally, the IRGC was given the portfolio. His advisors later decided that the best way to move forward was to hire a Russian scientist to head the effort. Once they were certain that Iran would become a nuclear power, they had no choice but to invest in a delivery system." General Zanjani paused. Janusz looked up from writing in the small notebook to urge him to continue.

"Three years ago, the IRGC began work on an indigenous Intercontinental Ballistic Missile (ICBM) called the Buraq, the name of the mythical creature that carried our great prophet to Jerusalem. This project was given the highest priority. The punishment for revealing any part of this program is automatic execution," General Zanjani said with a sigh.

"There are those in our country who believe the present regime has lost its way. They think Ayatollah Mashhadi is only interested in enriching himself. The most fervent followers of Imam Mahdi had long ago formed a secret society called the Hojjatieh. Imam Mahdi's return presents an obvious paradox for the position of a supreme leader," General Zanjani said.

"Can I have one of those?" Janusz said, pointing to his cigarette.

"I thought you don't smoke."

"I don't, but this is as good a reason as any to start." Janusz took the cigarette and placed it in his mouth. General Zanjani lit the tip with his lighter.

"As soon as members of the Hojjatieh were aware of the progress in these programs, they started to plot. Their efforts led to the election of President Azari, a prominent leader of their society. They then recruited sympathizers within the ranks of the IRGC. You may have already guessed that I too am a member of the Hojjatieh."

Janusz started choking on his cigarette and immediately moved to put it out in the ashtray. General Zanjani couldn't stop laughing. Janusz was not aware of the General's affiliation with the Hojjatieh, but he kept his mouth shut.

"One evening, there was a clandestine meeting nearby in Tehran. The Hojjatieh decided that the best course of action toward hastening the return of Imam Mahdi was to carry out a coup against Ayatollah Mashhadi. President Azari could then blame the supreme leader's assassination on the Americans. He would then seek revenge by ordering a preemptive nuclear strike on the continental United States."

Janusz could not believe his ears. None of the experts back home had predicted such a scenario. They had decided long ago that Iranian regime leaders were 'rational actors.'

"This is all very hard to swallow. Why would the plotters want to order a suicidal preemptive attack against America after their coup? Shouldn't they be worried about consolidating their victory?"

"You disappoint me, John. You're forgetting that the Islamic Republic of Iran is not a normal country. The very essence of this regime is centered on the return of Imam Mahdi. The Hidden Imam only returns when injustice in the world has reached a crescendo. If Iran attacks the United States with its nuclear weapons, your country will have no choice but to return the favor. That will be the very definition of an apocalypse that supporters of the Hojjatieh have been waiting for."

"You're fucking serious, aren't you? They really want to do this?"

"Afraid so, the only thing holding them back is a stable fuel for the Buraq. Once the solid fuel is ready, the Hojjatieh will carry out its coup and attack your country."

"Son of a bitch, what's the maximum range of the Buraq missile?"

"Fifteen thousand kilometers."

"That's enough—"

General Zanjani finished Janusz's sentence, "Enough to reach any point in the United States."

"Is there any way to stop them?"

"The only thing I can think of is to eliminate the head of the missile program. He is almost single-handedly responsible for our progress. He is our Sergey Korolev. His name is Dr. Abbas Esfehani Moghaddas. His colleagues call him *Ostad*, the professor."

Janusz took a deep breath to gather his thoughts. "How come I've never heard of this man before?"

"He is so crucial to the program that his identity is guarded more closely than the Buraq missile itself. Ayatollah Mashhadi was afraid that if his name became public, your government or the Israelis would attempt to kill him. It's against the rules even to mention his name in the same sentence as the word 'missile.'"

Before General Zanjani had finished speaking, Janusz knew he had no choice but to kill Dr. Esfehani before leaving Iran.

"Listen to me, General. I need to get close to Dr. Esfehani. Tell me about his daily routine. Where he works, where he lives, what he does for fun."

"It'll be difficult for you to get close to him without endangering your life."

"Why?"

"For one thing, he is always surrounded by at least ten

bodyguards, the most experienced men of the IRGC's Ansar Al-Mahdi VIP protection unit. There are guards stationed at his house and guards who travel with him wherever he goes. He is asked to provide a detailed itinerary any time he travels outside Tehran. I don't have anything for you now, but if you can hold on, I might be able to get you his home address. I'll send the information through our usual channels."

"That'll be satisfactory. I don't want to be rude, but I must get going. I'll be waiting for your email."

They stood up to embrace. When Janusz walked out, it was eerily quiet. The street was strangely devoid of pedestrians. It was a good omen. Within minutes, Janusz disappeared into the darkness.

33. DR. ESFEHANI'S HOUSE, LAVIZAN, NORTH EASTERN TEHRAN, IRAN

November 10

Two-meter-high concrete walls surrounded his gated house in the Lavizan section of Tehran. Inside, his wife, Zaynab, tended their lush garden. In the back, a large swimming pool with a patio was the setting for guests, including many in the IRGC high command. The guesthouse served as the barracks for the eight-man security detail keeping constant vigil over his loved ones.

The father of Iran's missile program had worked hard to provide the best for his family while also staying fit for his country. His streamlined physique was the result of a vigorous exercise regimen—a minimum of an hour spent hiking through the mountains surrounding Tehran every morning. His beard was short-cropped with no mustache. He was wearing the base military uniform, white slacks, a white belt, a white dress shirt, and white dress shoes. His insatiable drive to succeed was fueled by a desire to pave the way for the return of Imam Mahdi.

Dr. Esfehani had sacrificed numerous holidays in service to his country, but he had no regrets. He prayed five times a day and agreed with President Azari that Iran's greatest enemy was the United States. He had taken a personal vow to one day destroy the Americans with his long-range missiles.

He had grown up in a small brick house with a father who was a cobbler and a mother who was a homemaker. Math and chemistry were his favorite subjects in high school. He had enrolled in the chemistry program at the University of Isfahan when the revolution toppled the Pahlavi Monarchy, forcing him to abandon his studies. He had joined one of the numerous security committees that eventually combined to form the IRGC.

His first assignment during the Iran-Iraq war had been in the counter-intelligence division. He proved to be a capable officer who willingly risked his life at the front. Numerous secret assignments later, his career had taken an unanticipated turn in the middle of the war. His management abilities had propelled his name to the top of the list to lead Iran's nascent ballistic missile program. An independent missile force had become necessary after months of Iraqi missile attacks. Since the international community had been unwilling to help them, the IRGC was forced to develop its own capability. In the fall of 1984, Dr. Esfehani had headed a team of nine IRGC artillery specialists on a six-month training mission to Syria. The Syrians had agreed to train the Iranians on the Scud missile system, but they didn't provide them with the actual missiles.

Dr. Esfehani had used the opportunity to learn everything he could about the Scud missile system. Several months later, the North Koreans had made known their willingness to sell ten reverse-engineered Russian Scud missiles. They, however, had been unwilling to train the Iranians on the actual operation of the system. Dr. Esfehani had proposed combining the training provided by the Syrians and the actual missiles provided by the North Koreans to create an indigenous missile force for Iran. He had convinced his superiors that instead of using all the missiles provided by the North Koreans, it would be best to keep two for future research. That was the genesis for Iran's missile industry with its numerous research, support, and production facilities. Two decades later, his country controlled the largest inventory of missiles in the Middle East. Now they were working on the most important missile of them all, the Buraq ICBM.

Dr. Esfehani drove through the gate of his Lavizan mansion in an armored Mercedes SUV accompanied by three *Ansar Al-Mahdi* guards. It was a last-minute decision to surprise his wife for lunch. He was elated to see that his eldest daughter, Fatimah, had brought his two-year-old granddaughter and four-year-old grandson to visit.

"*Ya Abolfazl*, what do we have for lunch, dear ladies? My afternoon appointment was canceled. I thought I'd surprise everyone."

"We're so glad you could join us. Mom made her famous *khorest-e bademjan* (eggplant stew with meat). I sense you have some exciting news for us," Fatimah said. Dr. Esfehani had always been supportive of her desires for higher education. That's why he'd given his blessing for both Fatimah and her sister to study at Tehran University. Fatimah had chosen to become a stay-at-home mom after getting married, but that was beside the point. Despite his religious upbringing, there were few opportunities that he would deny his daughters.

"May Allah bless this family with eternal health! It's indeed a great time for us all, dear Fatimah. Let's just say that the arrival of Imam Mahdi is near. We're making tremendous breakthroughs in the program," Dr. Esfehani said. He was staring at a picture on the wall.

"It appears the years of sacrifices are finally paying off. We should celebrate with a family pilgrimage to the Shrine of Imam Reza," Fatimah said.

"I'd love to join all of you, but I don't have time. I'll arrange for your security detail to Mashhad. When you arrive at the shrine, we can pray together over the phone," Dr. Esfehani said.

"Ah father, it won't be the same without you. We'll all pray for your success," Fatimah said dejectedly.

After finishing his meal, Dr. Esfehani kissed his wife, his grandchildren, and his daughter goodbye. His security detail was waiting in the German SUV. He sat in the driver's seat and closed the door. As much as he despised the decadent ways of the West, there was nothing he enjoyed more than driving this marvel of German engineering.

34. THE IRGC MISSILE COMMAND HEADQUARTERS, WESTERN TEHRAN, IRAN

November 10

T he IRGC's Missile Command Headquarters, a nine-story building located in a secluded section of Tehran, didn't draw much attention to itself. The location was intended to make it difficult for overhead satellites to identify. Several layers of security controlled access to the facility. All electronic equipment was checked at a guard shack outside the main building. The employees used special badges issued for exclusive use at this facility.

Ashkan stared at a computer screen that displayed the locations of all of Iran's solid-fueled medium-range ballistic missiles. Named the Ashura, the missiles were capable of carrying a six-hundred-kilogram warhead to a distance of two thousand kilometers. Ashkan was in the middle row of a large control room that resembled NASA's Houston mission control center. This was the opening phase of an exercise simulating a full-scale retaliatory response to an Israeli strike on Iran's nuclear facilities in Natanz.

The exercise assumed that all command and control nodes had been completely cut off in the initial strike, making it impossible to receive orders from Ayatollah Mashhadi. In anticipation of this outcome, the supreme leader had preemptively issued a set of orders authorizing Missile Command Headquarters to launch a full-scale conventional attack against a number of Israeli military targets using the Ashura missiles. At the top of the target list was the Israeli nuclear facility in Dimona. Ayatollah Mashhadi had also authorized Brigadier General Akbar Javadpoor, Commander of the IRGC Aerospace Forces Missile Command, to strike US CENTCOM forward deployed facilities in the Persian Gulf, regardless of whether Israel had coordinated with the Americans.

Sitting directly to the left and right of Ashkan were missile command officers whose job it was to monitor the launch of shorter-range Shahab-2 and Ghiam missiles. Their orders were to destroy the facilities at CENTCOM forward deployed headquarters, Al Udeid Airbase, Qatar, and the headquarters of the US Navy's Fifth Fleet, located at Naval Support Activity, Bahrain. Ashkan was conducting the final checks with the missile launch control center in the western city of Kermanshah. Missile Command Headquarters was connected to the launch control centers that controlled the mobile and silo-based deployed missiles through dedicated fiber optic lines buried underground. As soon as he finished his conversation, Ashkan heard General Javadpoor through his headphones.

"With the recitation of this coded phrase, I'm ordering the exercise to begin. *Ya Ali Amir al Moemenin, Ya Ali, Ya Ali, Ya Ali.*"

Upon hearing the predetermined exercise code, *Ya Ali*, four times, Ashkan picked up the phone and pressed a button that sent a signal via dedicated fiber optic lines to the Kermanshah number 5 missile launch control center. This was the order, granting permission to destroy IDF Headquarters in Tel Aviv, Israel, with the Ashura. His comrades, each monitoring a different set of launch control centers in various regions of Iran, issued similar commands, authorizing the centers in their sectors to launch against their predetermined targets. Each sector controlled both mobile and silo-based missiles. The redundancy was necessary to increase the survivability of the missile force in the face of a coordinated air attack by a superior adversary. Computers integrated the data from the various terminals. The launches of different missile systems through-out the country were displayed on a large theater-size screen in front of the room. General Javadpoor and his Deputy analyzed the information on the main display.

General Javadpoor was promoted to this post follow-ing a two-year rotation as commander of the IRGC Aerospace Forces Air Defense Command. He was accustomed to running similar national-level exercises, aimed at strengthening Iran's integrated air defense system. His qualifications were not the reason President Azari had appointed him to this post. In add-ition to being the nephew of President Azari, the new missile commander was a member of the Hojjatieh, just like Ashkan. In reality, his job was to ensure the successful return of the Hidden Imam.

General Javadpoor turned toward his deputy and mo-tioned for him to come closer. The two men had served to-gether at the *Khatam-al Anbia* National Air Defense Command Headquarters during their previous assignment.

"Once you review the after-action report for this exer-cise, find out who performed the best at their assigned tasks. Pull those men aside for a special assignment where they'll prepare to simulate the launch of our ICBMs. We need to con-duct long-range missile drills against targets in the continental United States. Our Hojjatieh brothers in Sharif University have already developed the software for this drill."

"What about the intelligence office folks? Won't they be curious about why we are running ICBM drills?"

"No, they're aware Dr. Esfehani is working on this pro-gram. If anyone asks about the new drills, we'll tell them that we have to stay ahead of the research program to prepare for actual war. As a matter of fact, make sure to inform our section intelligence chief about this!"

"Yes, sir!"

35. IRGC REGIONAL MISSILE LAUNCH CONTROL CENTER, KERMANSHAH, IRAN

10 November 10

Kermanshah number 5 missile launch control center was located inside a mountain with over a hundred meters of rock protecting the control room. The room was connected to four separate mountain silos, each hiding a medium-range Ashura ballistic missile. The dense overburden rock and added concrete protected the precious instruments of destruction contained within. The hidden mountain facility contained a separate assembly area where the missile components arrived as a part of a kit. The components were then assembled before being placed inside a silo bay. A large tunnel with a railroad line allowed the maintenance crews to place the assembled Ashura missiles inside a cart that transported them to the silo bay where they were placed in a vertical position. A separate smaller tunnel contained the cables, wires, and fiber optic lines that allowed the missile command officers to control the missiles in the adjacent silo.

Entry into the control room was through a small opening that was sealed by a steel door. Inside the control room, filtered air was brought in via a series of air ducts connected to an airshaft leading out the side of the mountain. The shaft was disguised to resemble a natural mountain cavern. Supplemental gas tanks added oxygen to the filtered air, keeping the missile crews at a maximum state of alertness during their twelve-hour shift. With no access to an external light source, artificial lighting near 500 nanometers (nm) was provided by numerous green bulbs. The missile crews spent one month on and one month off shift inside the mountain. Their internal body clocks were set to Tehran central time, displayed on a 24-hour digital clock located at the top of each launch control console. The missileers were trained to keep rigid sleeping, eating, and exercise schedules to synchronize their circadian rhythms.

Hashemi was the senior launch control officer for bay 3. Sitting across his control console, he was the final link in the human chain responsible for launching the missile in the adjacent silo. His console contained a monitor panel, a radio set control, and a high-frequency transceiver. His control panel, where he would turn the key to launch the missile, was located directly above the program control panel. The telephone transmitter control was located next to an alarm monitor panel, and the missile status indicator occupied the center of the console, taking up the most space. This layout was probably familiar to previous generations of Minuteman III missile crews. The IRGC developers had copied the design from a schematic of an American Minuteman III launch control panel they had found online while conducting research into launch control room designs.

Hashemi waited for a call on the dedicated fiber-optic telephone connection that ran to his control panel from Missile Command Headquarters in Tehran. The order was required to authorize the launch of the Ashura missile in bay 3 for which he was responsible. For the purpose of this exercise, the commanding officer at headquarters was Ashkan. Hashemi picked up the phone to the cries of a prayer, "In the name of God, the most gracious and the most merciful, *Ya Hossein, Ya Hossein!*"

This predetermined order authorized the launch. While holding the phone with his left hand, Hashemi used his right to turn the key on the launch control panel. This motion illuminated a green button next to the key, which he pressed. Two and a half seconds later, the control panel indicated that the missile in bay 3 targeting IDF Headquarters in Tel Aviv had launched successfully.

He replied to Ashkan on the other end of the line. "The package for Tel Aviv is on its way." The men hung up their phones simultaneously.

36. THE IRGC MISSILE COMMAND HEADQUARTERS, WESTERN TEHRAN, IRAN

November 10

As soon as he hung up on Hashemi, Ashkan entered the information into his computer console. This updated the main control display for General Javadpoor. The other officers entered similar information into their consoles, providing a real-time display of activities for the missile forces commander in the control room. After forty-five minutes, General Javadpoor signaled the end of the exercise with the cry, "Ya Mohammad Rasool Allah." It was time for General Javadpoor to review the after-action report.

37. MALARD MISSILE RESEARCH FACILITY, WESTERN TEHRAN, IRAN

November 11

Siamak Pashaee had grown accustomed to being chauffeured around Tehran. This morning he was headed to the Malard research facility. His bodyguard was an employee of one of the new private security firms popping up like mushrooms in the Iranian capital. Siamak didn't trust the IRGC security force, Ansar Al-Mahdi. As a unit of the IRGC, they were ultimately answerable to one man, Ayatollah Mashhadi.

Sohrab Zoordar, Siamak's giant bodyguard, opened the door for the president's chief of staff. Sohrab waited by the car while Siamak walked toward the office of the program director. He instinctively checked his watch. He was five minutes early for his 9:30 a.m. meeting. He opened the main door with a badge and walked through a long hallway before taking the stairs to the second floor. When he arrived, the door to Dr. Esfehani's office was open.

"*Ya Abolfazl*! Come in, Siamak, I've been expecting you."

"*Besmillah Rahman Rahim*. Sir, allow me to skip the pleasantries and jump straight to the heart of the matter. President Azari is anxious about the progress of the Buraq Project. How much longer before the missiles are ready?"

"May Allah bless our beloved president with patience. As I've explained before, the work with missile fuels cannot be rushed. Allah is on our side and if it takes a bit longer for us to do this properly, so be it. You must relay what you learn today to your boss. Follow me."

Dr. Esfehani proceeded to guide Siamak out into the hallway. They rode an elevator down several hundred feet where
an underground passageway led to an assembly plant. Engineers
and technicians milled around missile components in various
stages of completion. They were too busy to notice Dr. Esfehani
and his guest.

"Siamak, the first thing to keep in mind is that the Buraq
missile requires the combined efforts of eight to ten separate
teams. Each team is composed of hundreds of experts scattered
across numerous facilities. One team is focused on the design
and construction of motor casings. For the first stage of the
Buraq, we're building a three-meter-diameter motor. A second
team is focused on the outer body components of the missile.
When complete, the entire system will be approximately forty-
five meters long. The teams will then decide which material
maximizes the range of the missile. The problem is that we
need to use extremely durable materials that can withstand the
stress of air friction and heat. Oftentimes, the very materials
that can withstand these external forces are heavy, requiring a
more powerful propellant to deliver the missile to the desired
distance."

Siamak took out a notebook from his coat pocket, furi-
ously writing down everything he heard.

"A third team is developing the guidance system to ensure an accurate flight path with a low circular error probable
(CEP). The CEP is an indicator of the delivery accuracy of a
missile system. It's the radius of a circle whose boundary is expected to include the landing point of half of our incoming missiles. The most accurate comparable missiles designed by the
Americans have a CEP of two hundred meters. Our system will
not be as accurate. However, given our intended use, we're not
too worried about accuracy. We're designing our own inertial
guidance system for the Buraq because GPS guidance is suscep-
tible to jamming. A fourth team is designing reentry vehicles
(RV) for our nuclear warheads. This work, like all the others,

focuses on minimizing weight as heavier warheads shorten the range of our missiles. I'm glad you're taking notes, the material will start to get complicated."

Siamak was now thanking Allah that he had an extra serving of *kale pacheh* for breakfast. This was a favorite Iranian dish consisting of an entire sheep's head cooked overnight. Once ready, meat was taken from the face, brains, eyes, and most prized of all, the tongue.

"A fifth team is developing the shields used to protect the missiles from the extreme heat generated by air friction during ascent and reentry. One mistake by this team and the warheads will disintegrate before reaching their targets. A sixth team is focusing on the integration of the various system components into a functioning three-stage missile. Finally, a quality assurance team checks the various components separately after they've been assembled."

Dr. Esfehani stared at Siamak, who was still taking notes. The director picked up where he had left off. "There are several other teams supporting the groups mentioned so far. I've left what, in my opinion, is the most important team for last. The propulsion team must design a safe and reliable fuel to power the entire system, weighing over one hundred thousand kilograms, to a distance of fifteen thousand kilometers. This is no easy feat, as you'll soon understand." Siamak checked his pockets for another pen.

"Several solid propellants were initially under consideration such as HTPB, PGN, and PBAN, each with different characteristics. What's significant is that all these fuels are extremely dangerous to mix. They must burn at a steady and predictable rate. We encounter problems whenever powerful fuels burn at high temperatures inside motor casings. The hot gases are emitted through the nozzle. The extreme temperatures cause corrosion of the conventional materials that are used to build motor casings and nozzles. Therefore, we've designed composite motors and nozzles to withstand extreme temperatures while maintaining structural integrity."

The technical aspects of the program were of no interest to Siamak. However, his boss had asked him to find out why the program was experiencing delays, so he was stuck.

"As I stated before, the fuel is the most critical component of the whole project. With most ICBMs, the propellant grain, also referred to as the fuel, takes up at least ninety percent of the total weight of the missile. It's therefore essential to maximize the efficiency of the propellant while reducing the weight of the overall system. For these reasons, success in rocket motor design depends heavily on knowledge of the burn rate behavior of the propellant under a variety of conditions. During the development of a new solid propellant, we must extensively test all burn rate characteristics under different temperatures, pressures, and conditions. To do so, we usually conduct what are called subscale and full-scale static motor tests. We'll return to this later." Dr. Esfehani said as one of his assistants handed him a bottle of water.

"Remember that the missile motor is the combustion chamber where the propellant is burned to produce thrust to power the missile. Missile motors burn one of two types of fuels, either liquid or solid. Most countries prefer to use solid fuels for their intercontinental missiles, given that solid fuels are usually more stable than liquid ones. They can also be stored inside the missile, ready to launch immediately. Liquid fuels, on the other hand, must be loaded into the missile just before launch. This makes liquid fuels less useful for wartime applications."

"What exactly is a static motor test, sir?" Siamak said.

"As I've stated, the missile motor is where the combustion of fuel occurs to produce thrust, which is the force that propels the missile forward. Therefore, if we test a missile motor without tying it down, it will fly off uncontrollably, killing everyone nearby. Instead, we can separate the motor from the missile, and tie it down to a test-stand, allowing us to ignite the fuel in a controlled environment. We then use various instruments to measure the performance of the propellant. The

Germans developed the basic methodology before World War II. Dr. Werner Von Braun enabled the Americans to develop their Saturn V rockets in preparation for the moon landings."

"What comes next?" Siamak said to hurry things along.

"The static motor tests are followed by a flight test of the entire missile. The subscale motor test is where a smaller motor than the one that will fly is used to test the characteristics of the propellant while it's tied down. We subsequently conduct a full-scale motor test. The motor here is the same size as the one that will be used on the assembled missile. Finally, we must test the fueled motor in flight under real-world conditions. At this step, we measure the effects of variables such as air friction, gravity, and atmospheric pressures at different altitudes while the missile is in flight."

"Hold on a second, sir," Siamak interrupted as he tried to catch up.

Dr. Esfehani continued talking, "The performance data during flight is sent back to engineers using what we call telemetry signals. Keep in mind, dear Siamak, that the process I've described must be replicated for three different motors because an ICBM is not a single-stage system. Rather, an ICBM is often a three-stage system that sheds the heavier first stage motor so it can fly further more efficiently. The later stage motors carry less fuel, and they too must be static tested on the ground at subscale and full-scale levels before their flight test."

Siamak's vision grew blurry as he tried to keep track of what Dr. Esfehani said.

"Okay, where were we?" Dr. Esfehani asked.

"You had just finished explaining solid missile motors and the process of testing them during subscale, full-scale, and full-system flight tests."

Siamak was certain Dr. Esfehani was trying to test him.

"Yes, yes. As I stated earlier, most countries prefer to use solid fuels for their ICBMs because they can be preloaded on the missile. The most efficient process is to mold the propellant grains directly inside the motor. As you can imagine, this is not an easy process. Remember that solid missile fuel is a hard, rubbery substance. The geometric shape that this substance is molded inside the motor determines the thrust characteristics and overall flight performance."

"But I thought you're procuring the fuel from abroad?" Siamak said. Dr. Esfehani continued talking without acknowledging him.

"To protect the casing surrounding the missile motor from the extreme temperatures that are produced during combustion, we apply a layer of special insulation to the internal lining of the motor. Therefore, it's essential that we ensure that the propellant mass bonds completely to the insulation layer when we cast our solid propellant inside the motor. We must also ensure that there are no surface cracks or bubbles in the propellant during the process because solid rocket motors can't be turned off once they are ignited. They burn until all the fuel inside the motor is consumed. The fuel is burned, starting at the exposed surfaces where the propellant is converted to hot gas exhaust. The exhaust is subsequently expelled from the motor through the nozzle. Because the amount of thrust is determined by the burning of exposed surfaces, unintended cracks open up new burning surfaces, causing motor pressure and thrust to increase. The higher thrust will cause the fuel to be consumed faster, which results in the missile straying from its intended target.

"Numerous unintended bubbles or cracks in the propellant will also cause the motor to become over pressurized and explode during flight. We may also encounter this problem at the periphery where unbonded areas between the propellant and insulation layer create exposed surfaces to the hot high-pressure gases in the motor. Once again, this phenomenon can increase the burn area of the propellant, unintentionally increasing thrust and pressure. This will lead to the problems already mentioned."

At this point, Siamak had been exposed to more information about rocket propulsion than he could digest in one sitting. Perhaps Dr. Esfehani recognized his fatigue when he finally ended his diatribe on missile propulsion.

"May Allah grant you the ability to absorb everything I've explained here today. I'll let you go so you can explain everything to President Azari. I'm sure you now realize that we cannot speed this process along without compromising safety, even if we are procuring our fuel from abroad."

Siamak shook Dr. Esfehani's hand. He then made his way to the vehicle for the hour-long drive back to the Presidential Palace.

38. OFFICE OF THE IRANIAN PRESIDENT, CENTRAL TEHRAN, IRAN

November 12

The IRGC officers entered the room one by one for the 10:00 a.m. meeting with President Azari. The first to arrive was the defense minister, IRGC Admiral Ali-Reza Abbasi. The commander of the IRGC, General Mohsen Jafarzadeh, followed him. A few minutes later, General Akbar Javadpoor, the IRGC missile commander, walked in wearing a Palestinian keffiyeh around his neck. Next to enter the room was a tall man with a goatee and glasses, new to these meetings. The man was dressed in a navy suit with an open-collar dress shirt and no tie. The last man to enter the room was General Mojtaba Vatanparast, commander of the IRGC Aerospace Forces.

This morning's meeting was inside the president's personal office. The room was analogous to the American president's Oval Office, except it was not oval. President Azari's office was decorated with a framed calligraphy parchment hanging on the main wall that read, "*Ya Fatimah Al Zahra*," referring to Fatimah from Zahra, the revered daughter of the Prophet Mohammad, the wife of Imam Ali, and the mother of Imam Hussein. To the left and right of the framed calligraphy were pictures of Ayatollah Semnani and Ayatollah Mashhadi. The whole room was painted white. To the right side of the president's work desk was a small entertainment area separated by potted plants. In the center of this area were two white leather sofas facing each other. A white leather chair in between the sofas was reserved for the president. The IRGC officers sat across one another on the sofa. They were all uneasy about something. Perhaps it was the fact that the only person who actually lived in this house was running late. President Azari would likely be late to his own funeral. No one dared speak these words out loud. Finally, the president arrived as they rose to their feet.

"Gentlemen, please sit down. Sorry to be late. I was in the sauna. I had to relax after my swim."

The President had ordered a complete renovation of his residence using three million dollars from the state treasury. The upgrades included a state of the art gym and an indoor swimming pool. He had also requested a luxury theatre to view the latest movies from abroad. When everyone was settled, an assistant came by with a tray of hot Persian tea.

Each man took a glass as the president called the meeting to order. "I've called you all here today so I can introduce Behnam. He is a physicist and an expert on nuclear war strategy at Malek Ashtar University. Behnam will be our lead planner for the nuclear war against the Americans. He's here to discuss EMP or, as the Americans call it, 'Electromagnetic Pulse.'"

Behnam picked up where the president left off. "Good morning, gentlemen. I've spent the last five years poring through all the available literature produced by American and Russian experts. Our goal is to create maximum damage with a limited number of nuclear warheads. Unlike the Americans, we don't have hundreds of nuclear weapons. We're also limited to twelve ICBMs, each tipped with a six hundred-kilogram fifty-kiloton yield explosive. We believe the best strategy is to use five of those warheads to deliver an initial EMP attack across the Southern United States. The remaining seven warheads will be aimed at their strategic cities of Washington, D.C., Philadelphia, New York, Los Angeles, San Francisco, and Seattle. We also aim to spread panic in America's heartland. For that reason, one of our missiles will target the Midwest city of Minneapolis, Minnesota."

The IRGC officers sipped their tea while listening intently.

"In 1962, the Americans exploded a nuclear bomb in the atmosphere high above the Pacific Ocean, some fourteen hundred kilometers away from the island chain of Hawaii. This explosion blew out streetlights, triggered telephone outages, and caused radio blackouts on the island of Oahu. This means that warheads detonated high above their targets are still effective. Our missiles will not have to travel that high—about a thousand kilometers will do. As a matter of fact, any warhead that can yield a one- to three-kiloton explosion will suffice. Our warheads will be designed specifically to maximize the production of gamma rays. These gamma rays interact with the earth's magnetic field in the upper atmosphere to produce the EMP effect."

"What does that mean, sir?" General Jafarzadeh asked Behnam.

"It means that there are three components associated with an EMP—the E1, E2, and E3 pulse. The E1 pulse travels at close to ninety percent of the speed of light, damaging things such as communications equipment by exceeding their voltage limitations. The E2 pulse happens more slowly than the E1, but it does not damage power grids. The E3 pulse is the slowest, but this is the one that affects the earth's magnetic field. The E3 will create huge currents on power lines that will destroy electric transformers and power plants. What is interesting is that Americans on the ground will not feel an EMP attack passing through their bodies. However, their smartphones, computers, TVs, radios, cars, and airplanes will no longer work. They will be unable to communicate with each other." Behnam paused to breathe. "Imagine the chaos that will ensue after such an event. A blow of this magnitude to the US telecommunications network, banking sector, and power grid will have devastating effects across the rest of the planet. We estimate that the resulting devastation will be of the magnitude that would necessitate the return of Imam Mahdi to bring about the new world order," Behnam said.

The IRGC officers shook their heads in disbelief. President

Azari wore a sheepish grin.

"Now, the Americans were smart enough to harden their military infrastructure early on to ensure effective command and control over their strategic nuclear forces in case of a Soviet EMP attack. Our EMP strike will not be sufficient to disrupt their response. Then again, we were never worried about their response, to begin with. We only want to deliver the first blow against the enemies of Islam. At that point, Allah willing, Imam Mahdi will defend our people," Behnam said.

"What happens then?" President Azari broke in.

"Sir, allow me to present the results of a study the Americans have produced. Several years ago, the Americans stood up an EMP commission in their congress to study the vulnerability of their country to an EMP attack. According to the findings, and I'm quoting now," Behnam took a piece of paper out of his coat pocket, "an EMP generated by a high-altitude nuclear explosion puts our society at risk of catastrophic consequences. A single EMP attack may seriously degrade or shut down a large part of the electric power grid in the geographic area of EMP exposure immediately. There is also the possibility of functional collapse of the electric grids beyond the exposed area. Ultimately, many people will die due to the lack of the basic elements necessary to sustain life in dense urban and suburban areas."

Behnam turned from side to side. They were eager to learn more.

"Now that we've established the necessity of incorporating an EMP component into our attack strategy, you may have doubts about our ability to penetrate their antiballistic missile defense system. We have an answer for that as well. Our research indicates that their ABM system is directed at threats over the North Pole. The Americans have not deployed any missile defense systems against incoming threats from the South. That's why the initial strike will focus on the Southern United States. When the power grid of the southern states is thrown into chaos, it'll have a domino effect that will wreak havoc on the entire North American grid, including Canada. We can consider Canada as an added bonus," Behnam said.

"How many Americans do you estimate will die as a result of this attack?" General Jafarzadeh interrupted once more.

"It is hard to say. These things aren't an exact science. However, if I were a betting man, I'd wager that at least eight to ten million Americans could die within the first month of the attack," Behnam replied.

Everyone in the room seemed pleased. President Azari was next to speak. "It so happens, gentlemen, that Dr. Pavel Yevchenko is an expert on creating nuclear EMP effects. That's not why we hired him originally, but when I approached him about the subject, he told me not to worry. Maximizing the effects of EMP explosions is one of his specialties. It appears Allah has a plan for everything. Now, if none of you gentlemen have any questions for Behnam or me, I'll adjourn this meeting. I must consult an expert on *estekhareh* for an important upcoming policy decision."

Estekhareh was a practice known in the West as bibliomancy. An expert flips open the Quran in a random fashion to use the first passage he encounters as the basis to decide a policy question. Certain clerics in Iran performed *estekhareh* in exchange for a hefty fee. Very few Americans were aware that policymakers in Iran made important national decisions in this fashion. That was a good thing. Their ignorance made it harder for them to predict the actions of the Iranian Government.

39. THE HOTEL ESPINAS, CENTRAL TEHRAN, IRAN

November 13

T he alarm went off at 6:00 a.m. Janusz had spent the previous day meeting with representatives of Pars Aluminum. They had taken him to one of their distribution centers in Tehran, a surprisingly modern facility. After the tour, Janusz and the managers of Pars Aluminum at lunch at Javan, one of the premier kabob houses in the Iranian capital. The managers of Pars Aluminum were affable enough despite their IRGC backgrounds. An investment with them would yield a handsome profit.

Janusz was not about to support this corrupt system.

The stock of Pars Aluminum had returned four hundred percent over the past three years and was likely to produce similar returns in the future. The problem was the blatant manipulation of the market. The network of former IRGC officers who managed Pars Aluminum and most other companies in Iran provided insider tips to their friends. They manipulated market prices, then bought large blocks of shares to profit on derivatives such as stock options. Any investment with these men was a safe bet. However, this was at the expense of the average Iranian, always defrauded by such schemes. Janusz was not about to support this corrupt system.

Upon returning to the hotel after his visit with the Pars Aluminum executives, Janusz opened an email from General Zanjani. The attachment contained the home address of Dr. Esfehani along with directions to the Malard research facility. He had already arranged his rental car. The hotel had procured a Mercedes sedan with tinted windows.

He drove out right after breakfast. Janusz navigated using paper maps. He did not want to type Dr. Esfehani's address into the local internet search engines. The choice of a luxury vehicle to navigate the traffic-infested streets of the Iranian capital had been a wise one. The Mercedes had responsive steering and comfortable seats. Nikolay Rimsky-Korsakov's *Scheherazade* played on the speaker system.

Dr. Esfehani's neighborhood was quiet at 8:00 a.m. Janusz drove by the front of the house twice before parking the car across the street. He turned the camera to face the front gate. He worked quickly to minimize the risk of detection by Dr. Esfehani's counter-surveillance team.

According to General Zanjani, the director was probably at his office at the moment. He decided to examine the property in search of a lapse in security. His surveillance camera, a tiny speck attached to the rearview mirror, monitored the entire street. The camera transmitted its feed to a geosynchronous satellite thirty-three thousand kilometers above in the sky. The feed then bounced back to a receiver in Janusz's cell phone. He was able to monitor Dr. Esfehani's house from the nearby Lavizan Park in real-time.

The Unit had purchased the satellite to enable real-time communications for field operators. This particular satellite covered an area from Europe to East Asia. It was one of three in a constellation that monitored the entire planet except for the extreme northern and southern latitudes. The cost, nearly a billion dollars, was covered by a group of hedge fund managers with connections to the Unit. They were willing to pay any price to guarantee America's safety. Janusz locked the car and made his way toward the park.

Tehran was famous for its parks. Former mayor Karbaschi had made a huge investment in them during the 1990s. It was part of the effort to counter the effects of air pollution that suffocated the city of fourteen million. It would have also helped if catalytic converters were mandatory for automobiles.

When he reached a secluded region of the park, Janusz pulled out his smartphone. He had brought some snacks from the hotel, including a chewy white pastry containing pistachios and almonds the Iranians called *Gaz*. He calmed himself by focusing on the chirping birds while monitoring his screen. As he drifted in and out of his thoughts about Jennifer, he spotted two cars approaching the target house.

It had to be Dr. Esfehani. There were at least eight men accompanying him. He saw four men in one vehicle and five in the other. The gate opened as the lead vehicle approached. Two men stood inside the gate with automatic rifles. The guards visually inspected the occupants of the first vehicle, then the second. When both cars were safely inside, the gate closed once more.

It was hard to tell how many men were inside the compound. Forty-five minutes later, the two cars reemerged. Janusz ran toward the rental. He jumped in and followed the convoy.

When the light turned red at the intersection of Taleghani and Vaseqi Streets, Janusz was three cars behind the second vehicle in the convoy. He could not be certain which vehicle the director occupied. He had a fifty-fifty chance, and he went for it.

After leaving the hotel garage, he had pulled over on a secluded street to place a locally purchased remote-controlled vehicle underneath his rental. He pressed a button on the control panel. A retractable arm lowered the remote-controlled vehicle on the asphalt. The vehicle carried a homemade bomb provided by a local asset. He picked up the control panel, steering the tiny car toward Dr. Esfehani's convoy.

The view from the camera inside the remote vehicle confirmed its location. He used his hand to wipe the beads of sweat on his forehead. He had learned to embrace fear over the years. Instead of letting the primal instinct paralyze him, he channeled the energy to do what he needed. He scanned the horizon one last time. Janusz pressed the red button with excitement.

The explosion was larger than anticipated. The blast startled him as the shock wave rattled his car. Then there was silence. A moment later, nearby motorists exited their vehicles. They were all shell-shocked. He cocked the SIG 226 before placing it behind his back. Without warning, the second vehicle in Dr. Esfehani's convoy created space for itself by ramming the car behind with sufficient force to create an opening. The driver quickly maneuvered out of danger. Did he blow up the wrong car? There was only one way to find out.

General Zanjani had provided a picture of the director in his last email. Janusz walked ever so slowly toward the demolished vehicle. He took a deep breath before opening the rear passenger door. The bomb had blown a hole in the floor of the passenger compartment. It had sprayed a decent amount of shrapnel inside the cabin.

Everyone inside was dead. The man closest to him in the back was holding his abdomen. It had ripped open, with the intestines spilling out into his hands. How could so much blood come out of one man? The nauseating smell of burning flesh forced him to breathe through his mouth. The second man in the back seat was holding a pistol in his hand. A mangled metal fragment was lodged in his forehead. Blood ran down his face and his clothes.

Janusz turned toward the front. The driver and his passenger had not fared much better. A piece of shrapnel had opened the back of the driver's head. Bits of brain oozed out onto his shoulder. A chunk of gray matter was dangling on the back of his seat. It would not be long before gravity pulled it toward the floor. He was reminded of *kaleh pacheh*, the Iranian breakfast made of sheep brains. All four men had microphones in their ears. *Fuck, Dr. Esfehani was in the other car!*

Janusz took care not to touch anything inside the vehicle. When the other motorists approached, he told them to go back. He was certain none of them would be able to identify him amidst all the confusion.

Moments later Janusz drove away before the police arrived. He searched frantically. The second vehicle in the convoy was nowhere to be found. It would be impossible to get another shot at Dr. Esfehani after the botched attempt. He decided to go back to the hotel. It was time to leave Iran.

Thirty minutes later, he was stuck in traffic. He pulled off the main highway, navigating the side streets for a shortcut. He cut through Felestine Street, headed north toward Keshavarz Boulevard, where the Hotel Espinas was located. Only a few more blocks.

The evening traffic had come to a standstill. Drivers fought for every inch of space on the road. Although ordinarily polite people, Iranians were quite aggressive behind the wheels of their cars. The light turned red as the intersection cleared out. He punched the accelerator, barely making it across.

The blinking lights of a motorcycle cop appeared in his rearview mirror. He swallowed hard as the officer motioned for him to pull over. It was best to play along. He placed the remote-control panel underneath the passenger seat. Officer Nehmati introduced himself in Persian.

"English, I only speak English," Janusz replied.

"*Agha Lotfan Tasdighe Ranandegeetono bedeen be man.*" *Please hand over your driver's license* the officer said.

"I'm sorry. I only speak English."

The officer spoke into his police radio. "Just pulled over a suspect that fits the description. He was blocking the intersection on Felestine Street. Please advise?"

"Unit 223, we're sending backup to your location!" came the crackling reply on the radio.

40. CANTON TRADING WAREHOUSE COMPLEX, SINGAPORE

November 13

Massoud sat in the back of the Lincoln Navigator while Quan drove. Quan was unusually large for a Chinese man, and he was probably more than a chauffeur. The Chinese military conducted business through a variety of front companies in Singapore. They arrived at a facility surrounded by a tall chain-link fence with barbed wire. The only entrance was through a gated guard shack. The guard raised the gate after inspecting Quan's identification. They drove to the front of a massive warehouse.

Someone finally opened the gargantuan sliding doors after a short phone conversation with Quan. Massoud stepped out of the vehicle while Quan remained seated. Three middle-aged Chinese men greeted him all at once.

"Good evening, Mr. Hosseinzadeh. Welcome to Canton Trading Company. My name is Mr. Chen. This is Mr. Chang and Mr. Bo."

"A pleasure to meet you," Massoud said eagerly as he walked over to shake their extended hands.

"Mr. Hosseinzadeh, my associates don't speak English. I'll translate for them when necessary. Let's walk to my office," Mr. Chen said.

The group proceeded to the back of the warehouse where row upon row of boxes were stacked to the ceiling. Massoud could only guess what was stored inside. More importantly, how much was the mystery merchandise worth? The far end of the facility contained several rooms. Inside one of them was a large table covered with an assortment of pastries and tea.

"Some tea for you?" Mr. Chen asked.

"Yes, please, I prefer black tea." Massoud replied.

A server poured tea into white porcelain China that came as part of a set. The man was dressed in a white coat and gloves. He poured three more teas for the hosts. On the table, there was a stack of white porcelain plates. The edges were rimmed with gold enamel. Massoud wondered why his hosts had gone to all this trouble for an informal warehouse meeting.

"This is fantastic, Mr. Chen. I was not expecting something so fancy."

"We Chinese have an ancient civilization like yours. Just because we're meeting in a warehouse does not mean we have no manners."

After nodding to acknowledge Mr. Chen's generosity, Massoud wiped his mouth before speaking. "On behalf of the Islamic Republic of Iran, I'd like to express my gratitude to you for facilitating this meeting. Is it safe to speak freely in this room?"

"This hangar is enmeshed with wiring that blocks electronic signals. We sweep for listening devices twice a day. Our cell phones, including yours, are stored in a locker in the hallway. Please speak your mind freely," Mr. Chen said.

"Very well. I'm interested in purchasing solid fuel for long-range missiles. I've been told you're the man to speak to." Massoud said.

Mr. Chen took a bite of his cookie without saying a word. When the silence became awkward, he replied, "What's the intended range of your missiles?"

"I've not been authorized to discuss details. I can only say we need enough solid propellant to deliver at least twelve missiles carrying a six hundred kilogram warhead over ten thousand kilometers," Massoud said.

Mr. Chen's face began to twitch although he was clearly trying to maintain a poker face. Mr. Chang and Mr. Bo both moved in their seats as they stared directly at him. It was highly unlikely that they did not understand English.

"Let me see if I understand you correctly. You want to purchase fuel for the PLA's ICBM? Not just for one, but for twelve missiles?" Mr. Chen asked.

Even though the men in this room were motivated by money, there was probably a limit to how much they were willing to risk. Nevertheless, Massoud had nothing to lose by taking a maximalist approach.

"Yes, Mr. Chen. We're interested in the propellant for your Dong Feng 31 missile system. We'll pay any price you deem reasonable."

The worst that could happen now was that they would tell him to get lost. Mr. Chen spent the next fifteen minutes conferring with his associates. Massoud could not determine what they were talking about. Oddly enough, their conversation seemed scripted.

"That's a tall order, Mr. Hosseinzadeh. If we help you, we make ourselves the target of the Chinese authorities, not to mention the Americans and Israelis. However, we're willing to sell what you need at a price of twelve million American dollars. The money needs to be deposited in an account we maintain at the Allies Bank of Singapore. These are our non-negotiable terms," Mr. Chen said.

Massoud pondered the terms. There was a possibility that his hosts would provide a defective product. That was a risk he had to take. If these men delivered on their promise, he would become the hero of the Iranian missile program. The only question was whether Dr. Esfehani would agree to the requested payment amount.

Massoud spoke up at once, "I need to confer with my superiors before I can agree to the twelve million. I—"

Mr. Chen cut him off before he could finish. "You have exactly twenty-four hours. If I don't hear back from you, please don't bother to contact us again."

"Thank you very much for your generosity," Massoud

said.

"Mr. Quan will drive you back to your hotel," Mr. Chen said.

Massoud grabbed his phone in the hallway before walking out to the Lincoln Navigator.

At around midnight, Singapore time, Massoud dialed his boss using a VPN. The connection was encrypted with proprietary IRGC software designed for secure international communications. Massoud explained that Canton Trading was willing to supply their needs for twelve million dollars. They had less than twenty-four hours to reply.

"Good work, Massoud! I'll authorize the wire transfer to one of our bank accounts in Singapore. You'll be designated the account holder with authority to transfer the funds to any account that Canton Trading provides."

Massoud dialed Mr. Chen the next morning regarding the payment. When he hung up, he imagined what it would be like to return as a hero. There was only one thing that was bothering him now. Dr. Esfehani and President Azari were about to destroy everything Ayatollah Mashhadi had done for his country. He needed to take care of some unfinished business when he returned to Tehran.

41. LOCAL POLICE STATION, TEHRAN, IRAN

November 13

The backup unit arrived within ten minutes. Officer Nehmati briefed another policeman as Janusz listened in. What profile did he fit? He had no choice but to go to the police station for questioning. He reached into the glove compartment to grab a small box with a cyanide pill inside. One of the officers suddenly spoke up in English.

"Sir, please come with me."

Janusz stepped out of his vehicle to walk over to the police cruiser. His hands were not cuffed as he was placed in the back seat. The drive to the police station was short. *Why did I push through that intersection? Maybe they were already onto me?*

The only silver lining was his cover as an Australian. If he had traveled here as an American, they would have accused him of working for the CIA regardless of the facts. They arrived at a station for the *Nirouye Entezami Jomhourieh Eslami* (NAJA), the *Iranian police*. Unlike police forces in most countries, their uniforms resembled that of the military. They wore light green dress shirts with black nametags pinned over the right breast pockets. A slide-on epaulet decorated each shoulder, indicating their rank. The two officers now walking with Janusz had attained the rank of captain. Their pants were also dark green, and black dress shoes covered their feet. Oddly enough, green baseball caps adorned their heads instead of the common police caps worn in most countries.

They escorted him to an empty interrogation room where he was seated behind a desk. A small window with bars on the outside allowed sunlight into the room. As usual, pictures of Ayatollah Semnani and Ayatollah Mashhadi adorned the brick walls. Deep inside Iranian territory, Janusz entertained no thoughts of escape. A small camera near the ceiling along the left corner of the room was staring straight at him.

Janusz slid a hand into his pant pocket, surreptitiously opening the box to place the cyanide pill between his fingers. He drew his hand back out in a natural motion to cover his mouth while he pretended to yawn. He placed the cyanide pill between his right cheek and gum line. It was odd feeling safer with a poison pill in his mouth. He suddenly remembered his dead brother Ben. He had no choice but to make it out of here alive. After about thirty minutes, a bearded man wearing the same uniform as the others came into the room. The man was a lieutenant colonel. He sat in front of Janusz speaking fluent English.

"Do you have your passport with you?"

Janusz slid his passport across the table. The colonel studied the first few pages while leafing over the rest.

"So, you're Australian. Do you think that gives you the right to break our laws?"

"I'm not sure I understand, sir," Janusz replied, unaware of what the colonel was talking about.

"You've been detained for running a red light and blocking a major intersection in Tehran. Do you act the same way in your own country?"

"No sir, but—"

"But what? You think this is a lawless society? What gives you the right to break our laws? Perhaps you have no respect for Iran?"

The colonel was obviously trying to bust his balls. He decided to play along. "That's not the case at all. I have tremendous respect for Iran and its laws. Your country also has aggressive drivers. They constantly honk at anyone who holds up traffic. I tried to stop at an intersection waiting for the light to turn. The traffic behind me was relentless. I had no choice but to run the light in fear that some crazy driver from behind would attack me."

The colonel seemed embarrassed. "Yes. Unfortunately, our citizens don't always obey the traffic rules." Both men stared at each other before the colonel spoke once again. "Why are you in Iran?"

"I'm here on business. I want to invest in your country, specifically Pars Aluminum. Have you heard of it?"

Janusz was sure that he had. The managers of Pars Aluminum had told him that a major portion of the police officers retirement fund was invested in their company.

"Please, you can come up with a better excuse. I will ask you one more time. What are you doing in Iran?"

"Sir, you've made a big mistake. I've been invited here as a guest of Hessam Jafaari. We've discussed a number of investment opportunities. I was taking the day off to travel around Tehran before I was detained by one of your men for an offense that is quite common here," Janusz said before placing a business card on the table. "This is Mr. Jafaari's contact information. Please call him immediately so I can go back to my hotel."

The colonel's eyes widened at Janusz's demanding tone. Hessam Jafaari was a respected former general in the IRGC. He was also one of the most connected men in Iran with personal ties to Ayatollah Mashhadi. The colonel picked up the business card as he left the room to make the appropriate inquiries. He returned a few minutes later, skin pale and head slightly bowed.

"Mr. Phillips, I'm so very sorry. My men have made a terrible mistake. I hope you'll accept my apology. Mr. Jafaari just informed me that you are here to make a large investment in our country. You're free to leave as soon as you like."

This had to be the world's greatest coincidence. He had not been detained for the assassination attempt on Dr. Esfehani. The police must not have found anything in his car that made them suspicious. As far as he could tell, his life was not in immediate danger—at least, not yet. He was, however, curious as to what had happened. He decided to push his advantage to find out more.

"I'll accept your apology on one condition."

"Yes please, what is it?"

"Why did you detain me? It was obviously not because of the traffic violation, which is all too common here."

"Officer Nehmati did, in fact, stop you for running a red light. We have to do that every once in a while. When you spoke in English, he called our control center. They asked him to keep you until backup arrived. You see, we're searching for a British man who has stolen antiquities from our country."

Was the colonel telling the truth? What were the odds that the Tehran police were searching for a British antiquities thief on the same day as his attempt on Dr. Esfehani? It would be foolish to ask more questions.

"I appreciate your honesty. If you don't mind, I'd like to go back to my hotel," Janusz said.

"Of course. Please wait outside, and one of my men will escort you to your vehicle."

In the hallway, Janusz sat down on a chair nestled against the wall. He cupped his hands under his mouth to rest his chin. He immediately spat out the cyanide pill before breathing out in celebration of cheating death. This detention could have gone very badly had he not kept his composure or used his connection with Jafaari. The rush of adrenaline made his hands shake. Tomorrow was going to be his last day in Iran. It could not come fast enough.

42. 101 COLLINS STREET, MELBOURNE, AUSTRALIA

November 14

J anusz spent the entire return trip on the Boeing 747 trying to figure out how to stop the nuclear attack against his country. Despite his fatigue, he scheduled the briefing with the Unit as soon as he landed. Every passing second meant Dr. Esfehani's team was one step closer to his Armageddon.

Everyone was present except for James Black and Ed Wright, who were on assignment in Singapore. A secure VTC link had been established with headquarters in Herndon. Janusz sat in the center of the conference room, staring straight into the camera. Over the next half hour, he relayed what he had learned from General Zanjani.

"I believe it's impossible to eliminate this man using traditional methods at his point," Janusz said.

"So what are you saying? Are we supposed to let these zealots start a world war?" Stan said.

"Stan is right. There has to be a way to kill this man in Iran," Tony said.

"With all due respect, we're talking about the Iranian capital, for Christ's sake. The city is monitored around the clock by cameras," Janusz said.

"Then what do you have in mind?" Tony said.

"As I stated earlier, we won't be able to get to this man

using traditional methods. You may be aware that a missile program requires lots of testing in order to succeed. Simply put, accidental explosions are likely to occur during research," Janusz
said as he leaned into the table.

"Please continue," Tony said.

"What if we were to supply the program with an unstable
ingredient?" Janusz said.

"How do you propose we do such a thing?" Stan said.

"What better time for us to purchase a company that sup-
plies missile fuels!" Janusz replied.

"What if they've already found a supplier?" Tony said.

"Then we'll buy them out," Janusz said.

43. CANTON TRADING WAREHOUSE COMPLEX, SINGAPORE

November 16

The phone rang for several minutes.

"Hello," Mr. Chen said.

"Hi sir, my name is Morteza Khakpoor. May I have a minute of your time?" came the reply.

"How can I help you, Mr. Khakpoor?"

"I'm with Rostami Partners, a company in Dubai."

"Yes, I've heard of you."

"I'm interested in purchasing your company."

Janusz, playing the role of Morteza Khakpoor, had contacted Mr. Chen after reviewing the transcript of a phone conversation between him and Massoud. James and Ed had intercepted the call during their assignment in Singapore. The Unit was also aware that the Chinese government was conducting one of its periodic anti-corruption campaigns. Several of Mr. Chen's contacts in the PLA had been arrested and thrown in jail.

"Mr. Khakpoor, are you by any chance in Singapore?"

"Yes, I am."

"Tell you what. Why don't you meet me tonight at our facilities at the harbor? We can discuss this matter in private. I'll text you the address."

◆ ◆ ◆

Janusz arrived at the gate of the Canton Trading facility at 9:00 p.m. Despite the heavy rain, the guard motioned for him to roll down the window.

"The dock is closed, sir. You must turn around," the man said.

"My name is Morteza Khakpoor. I'm here for Mr. Chen," Janusz replied.

The guard walked back to the shack to make a call. He hung up and approached the window once more, "please proceed to the large warehouse at the end of this road."

It was almost impossible to navigate through the torrential rain that fell mercilessly out of the sky. The main door of the warehouse was already open when he arrived. The guards searched him for weapons, then escorted him to an office in the back. Janusz shook hands with his host before taking a seat. The rain outside was beating faster now.

"Mr. Khakpoor, what's your interest in Canton Trading?"

"I'll be frank with you, sir. We're a major supplier of contraband goods to Iran. We want to expand our operations, especially in the arms business. We're aware of your access to the Chinese defense industry," Janusz said.

"Iran is also a heavily sanctioned country. All aspects of your potential dealings with them will come under tight scrutiny by a multitude of international organizations."

"We're aware of the pitfalls. But a greater risk means a greater reward."

"No problem, I'll consider a reasonable offer for my company." Mr. Chen said.

Janusz had already done his homework on Canton Trading. Even though they were not a publicly traded company, the Unit had been able to get an estimate for their annual revenues over the past five years. With average revenue of six million dollars, Janusz valued the company at six times its earnings. That came to thirty-six million dollars. There was also a downside. Given the level of scrutiny from Chinese officials, Canton Trading would have to shut down its operation very soon.

"I'm prepared to offer you twenty million dollars." Janusz said. That was a lie. HRC was willing to pay much more for Canton Trading.

"I'll accept an offer of twenty-five million."

"Done! There is one more thing." Janusz said.

"What is it?"

"My offer is contingent upon your delivery of all orders presently under contract. This means you must call Massoud Hosseinzadeh to inform him of the time and place where you'll deliver the fuel he is expecting." Janusz said.

Mr. Chen's mouth flew open.

"How did you know about this deal? It was supposed to be a secret."

"This deal is the very reason that I contacted you. Massoud had originally approached us with his predicament. A few days ago, I received a call from Massoud informing me that he had found a supplier in Singapore. I then researched the names of companies involved in such work. Canton Trading was at the top of the list. I guessed that you might be the supplier Massoud had mentioned. I decided to call you on a hunch. I took a chance in mentioning the deal. My gamble has paid off," Janusz said.

Mr. Chen remained quiet, staring coldly at Janusz.

"I apologize for tricking you, sir. If you're interested, the offer for twenty-five million still stands. One more thing, you cannot tell him that your company has been sold until after this deal is completed. I don't want him to get nervous."

"What about the money the Iranians want to pay us for the delivery of the fuel?"

"You can keep that," Janusz said. "Where will the transfer occur?"

"We have a facility in Sharjah."

"Great. I'll accompany you there and will remain in the back until the transaction is complete. Is the fuel on its way?"

"No, it's sitting inside the storage hanger across from us."

"Excellent. My colleagues will handle everything going forward. Please inform your employees that they must leave this facility at once."

A half-hour later, Mr. Chen was ready to go home. After driving past the guard shack, he dialed his wife through the Bluetooth. A voluptuous blond named Laura, he had met her at a party thrown by an Australian business associate. Mr. Chen instructed Laura to start packing. They were moving permanently to his seaside castle on the Isle of Man. She could finally escape the humidity in Singapore. Laura was ecstatic, asking what finally changed his mind.

"I sold the company. We have more than enough for the rest of our lives."

"Jesus, I thought you said you might lose everything soon. What the hell happened?"

"We found an Iranian buyer to take over the business. Let him worry about the Chinese and American Governments."

44. MALARD MISSILE RESEARCH FACILITY, WESTERN TEHRAN, IRAN

November 17

T
he Iranian-made Samand automobile pulled into an empty spot behind the main administrative building. It was 8:52 a.m., and he had eight minutes to spare. This was Massoud's first trip to Malard since returning from Singapore. It would not be long before he was running the place as chief engineer. He scanned his badge at the entrance door, and then walked inside, down a long hallway and up a flight of stairs. He knocked on an open door with a gold label that read "Dr. Abbas Esfehani Moghaddas."

"*Ya Abolfazl*! Come in, Massoud, come in. I've been bragging to everyone that I'm so lucky to have you on my team. It won't be long before we celebrate the destruction of America." Dr. Esfehani said.

Massoud was annoyed with Dr. Esfehani for being so kind this morning. He would have preferred for his mentor to be less receptive.

"May Allah grant you good health, Massoud! Canton Trading called us yesterday. The fuel will be delivered on November 25th in Sharjah."

"What happens next?" Massoud said.

"We make the final preparations before the Hidden Imam's arrival."

Massoud stared at his boss, *you're such an arrogant ass.*

"Ostad, we still have lots of testing to conduct before the

Buraq is ready for production. Isn't all this talk a bit premature?"

"Not so, dear Massoud. The composites team made a spectacular breakthrough while you were in Singapore. As a matter of fact, we're currently assembling twelve Buraq ICBM motors, ready to be fueled as soon as we receive our propellant in Sharjah."

"But sir . . . " Massoud said.

"As I mentioned to you already, President Azari has been breathing down my neck for several months. We don't have time to take all the precautions the Americans follow in their program. We can get the same results as the arrogant Yankees in a fraction of the time. Destroying the Great Satan and its Zionist lackey will be my greatest legacy, not this missile program."

"Of course, Ostad!"

"Remember, we also have to worry about the Americans destroying our facilities. That's why we've moved our assembly plant inside Barjamali Mountain."

"Wise decision, sir."

"The Americans have a variety of sensors on their satellites that can detect the heat signatures and telemetry signals of an ICBM launch as soon as it occurs. We know this because they used their TACKSMAN I and II facilities here in Iran to spy on Soviet missile tests in the 1970s. I've decided to forgo a full-system flight test before launch. If they discover our progress, they'll deploy their defensive missiles in Europe, negating our first strike capability."

"But how can you have confidence in our systems? How can you be sure our ICBM's will reach their destination without tests?" Massoud said.

"May Allah grant you eternal patience—I'm getting to that. We've made extensive use of the dynamic test tower that was recently completed near the city of Shahrud in Semnan Province. The tower provides a platform for holding our three-stage Buraq missile, fully assembled and fueled, to simulate the vibrations generated when engines are fired. This allows us to determine the Buraq's structural dynamic characteristics under conditions simulating flight configurations as much as possible."

"When did all this happen?" Massoud said.

"You didn't have a need to know until now. As I was saying, electrically powered shakers induce vibration modes in the rocket so its elastic deformations and structural damping characteristics can be determined. We conducted our dynamic tests in three phases using the model developed by Dr. Von Braun for the Americans. During the first phase, we tested the system as a whole with all three stages. The reentry vehicle and warhead were stacked together to simulate a full-system launch. In the second phase, we conducted a test as though the first stage had jettisoned while the second stage was firing. Finally, in phase three, we tested just the third stage with the reentry vehicle and warhead on top. Are you following?"

"Yes, Ostad."

Massoud made mental notes of the various aspects of the program he needed to be aware of when the time came. Then again, all of Dr. Esfehani's notes would be at his disposal once he became the new program director.

"Good, let's move on. The next thing we did after conducting the dynamic tower tests was to flight test each of the Buraq's three stages separately using a previously developed propellant that is not as powerful as the one you've acquired for us. We gave a different name to each stage, officially announcing that we were testing a single-stage, medium-range ballistic missile. We launched from Tabriz into the Indian Ocean where our ground stations and ships collected the telemetry to make sure that the missiles functioned properly. We gathered the data and reviewed the results expeditiously. Then, we announced the test of a civilian space launch vehicle using solid fuels."

"Oh yes. I remember reading that report in the news while I was in Singapore," Massoud broke in.

"Instead of a reentry vehicle, we mounted a satellite on top of our rocket and launched it into space. Our trick was to name the civilian space launch vehicle using the same term we use for our secret military one. In other words, we called it the Buraq Space Launch Vehicle to confuse the Americans. They'll wonder whether the Buraq program is an ICBM or a civilian space launch vehicle."

"That's brilliant, Ostad!"

"I know. The final part of the program that I want to tell you about pertains to systems reliability testing. We used the Bayesian method or 'pseudo trials,' as the Americans call them."

"Yes, I'm familiar with it."

"Good. A Bayesian reliability assessment mixes data from all of our critical data sources: system, subsystem, and component level tests. The method combines data logically via the repeated application of inductive mathematics. We based our Bayesian prior reliability estimates on the subsystem trials of each stage of our missile. We added data from design analysis, modeling, and simulation processes. We also included data from earlier tests of similar systems like the Ashura MRBM and other supporting information from our entire missile program. We combined our stockpile of historical data with the judgment of our engineers to gain a level of confidence in the reliability of our full Buraq Missile system.

"The Bayesian methodology allowed us to use increased reliability testing at the subsystem level instead of full-scale testing for system reliability. We used quality control measures that provided reliable data from our subsystem tests, providing a high degree of confidence in our results, and I'm certain that we designed and implemented reliable subsystem tests."

"Ostad, I'd feel better if we were able to conduct at least one full-system flight test before we carry out a nuclear attack against the Americans. However, given our time constraints, the Bayesian method will have to do, I suppose. Is there anything you need me to do at this point?"

"Yes, get some rest. We have lots of work in the days ahead."

"You can count on me, Ostad."

"May Allah grant you success!"

After shaking hands, Massoud walked back to his vehicle in the parking lot. He wondered how much his salary would increase when he was put in charge of the IRGC's missile program.

45. CANTON TRADING WAREHOUSE COMPLEX, SINGAPORE

November 17

D r. Nathan Anderson was mild-mannered and preferred to wear contact lenses to avoid the stigma of being labeled a nerd. Sporting blond hair with piercing blue eyes, he was average in most respects, including his height and build. The only thing not average about him was his intelligence, once measured at a 185 IQ. Dr. Anderson was not religious, but he compensated for it by devoting his life to the cause of keeping America safe. He grew up dreaming of a day when he would help launch rockets into space. He graduated from MIT's Aeronautics and Astronautics engineering program with a concentration in space propulsion.

Dr. Anderson spent years working as a propulsion expert with a defense contractor where he was in charge of maintaining the US Air Force's Minuteman III ICBMs. He then transitioned to the CIA where he was head of the analytic branch evaluating the missile capabilities of hostile nations. It did not take long for the risk-averse bureaucratic nature of the CIA to dampen his spirits.

Barely a week after he quit his job at the Agency, Dr. Anderson received a call from a former colleague, asking him to contact a private equity firm in Herndon, VA. The interview with HRC was the answer to his prayers. He was hired as a consultant on "special projects."

Dr. Anderson was excited about his first trip to Singapore.

In anticipation of the brutal humidity, he wore his pink short-sleeve polo with white dress pants. As he rode down the highway with Janusz in a red Ferrari 458 Italia, he felt like Don Johnson in an episode of *Miami Vice*. Once inside the Canton Trading dockyard, they drove to the main warehouse. As they walked around HRC's newest acquisition, Janusz finally revealed his assignment.

"What do you think?" Janusz said.

"It's a huge warehouse. What exactly are we doing here?"

"We own all this. Here's the deal. The Iranian Hojjatieh society wants to place a nuclear warhead on an ICBM. They plan to overthrow the supreme leader in order to launch a surprise nuclear attack against the US. How is all this grabbing you?"

"If I didn't know any better, I'd say it sounds like the plot of a novel."

"This is where you come in. We now own the most critical component of Iran's ICBM supply chain. You follow where I'm going with this?"

"Sabotage?"

"Precisely! I need you to study the Chinese propellant and figure out a way to create an 'accidental' explosion."

"I'll do my best."

"Excellent! Let's walk around so you can familiarize yourself. You'll be working here until you finish. Hazmat suits are available for the volatile substances."

Dr. Anderson spent two full days examining the DF-31 ICBM propellant. There were separate containers for the oxidizer, fuel, and binder needed to power the Iranian ICBMs. His epiphany struck like a bolt of lightning. When he was finished, he called Janusz.

"This is a quick rundown of what's going on. The main difference between solid and liquid propellants is that with the solids, the oxidizer and fuel are bonded together using a rubbery binder that keeps the mixture intact. The fuel is then cured into a solid and cast inside the motor where it'll be ready to be fired on a moment's notice. With liquid fuels, the oxidizer and fuel are kept in separate tanks before they are pumped into the combustion chamber when the missile is ready to be fired. Since our solid fuel must be cast and cured inside the missile motor we cannot as yet mix the materials we're providing the IRGC. They'll mix, cast, and cure the ingredients themselves. With any luck, they'll experience a huge bang when they put everything together," Dr. Anderson said.

"What if they don't?" Janusz said.

"I've done several things to ensure that they do. The essential element for a successful solid-fuel motor function is the burn rate. If the burn rate is not steady, then too much pressure is produced inside the motor, leading to a disastrous explosion. I made a slight change to the oxidizer batch along with the raw materials we're providing. The change should result in an unsteady burn rate that increases the motor pressure. I also tweaked the amount of burn rate catalyst they'll use to cause a burn rate spike that'll lead to an increase in motor pressure. I tampered with the igniters provided by the Chinese. The igniter is what initially begins the chemical reaction when the motor is fired."

"Is this what you talk about with women?" Janusz said.

"Not quite. Fortunately, I remembered that a premature ignition is what caused the Nedelin Catastrophe in 1960, the worst disaster in the history of the Soviet missile program. That explosion caused seventy-two fatalities, including the head of the Russian ICBM program, Chief Marshal Mitrofan Nedelin. When the IRGC mixes the materials I prepared, they should get a result similar to the Russians back in 1960. Can we trust Canton Trading to deliver our goods?"

"I'll be in Sharjah with Eric when they make the delivery. We'll keep an eye out to make sure Mr. Chen and his men do what they're supposed to."

◆ ◆ ◆

Janusz shook Dr. Anderson's hand and called Mr. Chen to arrange the fuel delivery. It was too early to celebrate. He decided to do one last thing before leaving for Sharjah.

"What's wrong, Janusz? I thought you said no more calls until this mission is complete," Jennifer said.

"That's true, but I've been doing a lot of thinking."

"Oh boy, here it comes."

"Hear me out now. It's taken a long time, but I finally realize you're the only one for me. I think Ben would've told me the same thing if he were still alive. I hope you'll consider—"

"You already know the answer, but there is a better way to do what you're trying to do," Jennifer said.

"Yes, of course, and I want to do it properly and in person. Let's just say I wanted you to hear this from me just in case—"

"Don't you dare complete that thought. Get the job done and ask me in person. At that time, I'll give your proposal the consideration it deserves. Are we clear, Mr. Soltani?"

"Crystal!"

"Oh, and Janusz?"

"Yes, ma'am?"

"I'll expect you to have addressed the gambling issue when you get on your knees."

46. MASSOUD HOSSEINZADEH'S APARTMENT, NORTH EASTERN TEHRAN, IRAN

November 17

S itting in the living room of his luxury high-rise, Massoud was conflicted about what he should do. Although Dr. Esfehani was responsible for the miraculous accomplishments of the Iranian missile program, none of it would have happened without the support of Ayatollah Mashhadi. After all, it was the supreme leader who had nurtured the program from the start by providing a blank check. Despite the need to expedite the return of the Hidden Imam, it would be foolish to do so at the expense of the supreme leader, a man who had done a great deal for his people. Massoud had been wrong about this all along. Instead of going to the Americans for extra cash, he should have reached out to the IRGC-IO from the beginning. If anything, it was Ayatollah Mashhadi who was most capable of leading the way to the return of Imam Mahdi. The more he thought about it, the more he was convinced that Dr. Esfehani and President Azari were traitors.

Massoud decided to take matters into his own hands. By saving the life of Ayatollah Mashhadi, he would be rewarded as the director of the missile program. He picked up the phone to call a friend at IRGC-IO. Within minutes, the call was transferred to another office, and he was on the line with Colonel Ramazani's secretary. Massoud was asked to come to the IRGC-IO Headquarters in Dowshan Tappeh.

◆ ◆ ◆

Massoud was having second thoughts about the meeting. Sweat ran down his back all the way to his boxers. He rehearsed the speech in his head as he rode the elevator to the top floor. He passed the commander's office, Katkhodah Lankarani, on his way to see Colonel Ramazani. He was a few minutes early, and the office door was closed. He took a seat along the wall outside. At 2:45 p.m., Colonel Ramazani opened the door. Inside his office, pictures of Ayatollah Mashhadi were everywhere. One such picture showed Colonel Ramazani sitting on the floor eating dinner with the supreme leader. It was still customary for traditional Shi'a families to eat food on the floor instead of on a table. It implied that the family, no matter how wealthy, had not been corrupted by Western culture.

"Welcome home, Dr. Hosseinzadeh!"

"Please call me Massoud."

"Very well, Massoud. You're probably aware I follow your progress quite closely. As a matter of fact, two of my men were on special assignment in Malaysia and Singapore when you were busy searching for a supplier for our missiles."

"Yes, of course. I spoke with one of them about the disappearance of Javad Pirnia. Has Javad been found?"

"Don't concern yourself with such matters. My men will locate him sooner or later. How is everything coming along?"

"We're on the cusp of success. We found a supplier in Singapore who has agreed to supply us with the PLA's DF-31 fuel."

"I thought solid propellants are not mixed until they're ready to be bonded to the motor?"

"That's correct, Colonel. They're sending us the fuel and oxidizer separately. We'll mix and test everything over the coming days at our hangars. Dr. Esfehani and all the engineers will be present at every step along the way."

"Excellent! Now, what brings you to my office?"

"Given the sensitivity of the topic, I was hoping we could discuss this matter in a secure facility?"

"We have a room below ground, reserved for such delicate matters. I'll make the call right now," Colonel Ramazani said as he picked up the phone. Within minutes, they were in the elevator, heading down to the mezzanine level where the IRGC-IO maintained a secure floor. This part of the building was impenetrable to electronic signals. Massoud was startled to find another man sitting by the wall when they entered.

"This room is usually reserved for the director's morning briefings. It's quite safe to discuss any topic on your mind," Colonel Ramazani said.

Massoud stared at the man sitting against the wall.

"Allow me to introduce my assistant, Hassan Hashemi. Anything you want to say, you can say in front of him. Please proceed."

There was no going back once he opened his mouth. Anyone associated with the Hojjatieh, including Dr. Esfehani, would be arrested and executed. Let the chips fall where they may.

"Colonel, I've come to share some disturbing news. I do so in the hope of saving our dear supreme leader. The Hojjatieh is a secret society founded in 1953. It went underground for a number of years after the revolution, in response to Ayatollah Semnani's edict. There was resurgence in membership in the early 1990s. A direct result of increasing dissent between the various factions of the regime. My father was also a member of the Hojjatieh. He took me to their meetings when I was a child. For most of its existence, the society has concentrated on curbing the growth of the Baha'i faith."

Colonel Ramazani's face did not betray any emotions. He calmly shifted in his seat as Massoud spoke. "The goals of the Hojjatieh have evolved since the election of President Azari. He dominated the meetings within a few months of taking power. His rants always berated our clerics, emphasizing how they were no longer interested in ushering forth the reign of Imam Mahdi."

Massoud paused to gauge his audience.

"I'm listening," Colonel Ramazani said.

"There are many cells within the Hojjatieh; no one knows exactly how many. Once President Azari took office, many high-ranking IRGC officers started attending our meetings. Within a few weeks, Ali Reza Abbasi, Mohsen Jafarzadeh, Mojtaba Vatan-parast, and Akbar Javadpoor had all joined."

Colonel Ramazani's face was no longer expressionless. He tightened his jaws and stood up. His left eye twitched as he bore into Massoud.

"I tried not to let the sudden popularity of the Hojjatieh distract me from my work. Then, one day, Dr. Esfehani pulled me aside. He told me that the Hojjatieh was fed up with the current leadership. He declared that the IRGC missile program would be the key to the return of Imam Mahdi. They had decided that the best way to set the stage for the return of the Hidden Imam was to provoke a nuclear conflict with the Americans. Twelve nuclear-tipped ICBMs would usher in the arrival of the Twelfth Imam."

Colonel Ramazani furrowed his brows in confusion, "how did you expect to pull this off?"

"I left the most unfortunate part for last. The plan is to recruit several assassins from the *Vali-e Amr* unit to storm into Ayatollah Mashhadi's office to execute him. The blame for this crime will be placed on the Americans. President Azari will then retaliate by launching a nuclear attack. I'm here to tell you that once Dr. Esfehani has the fuel, the plan will be implemented immediately," Massoud said.

"I don't know what to say. I'll—" Colonel Ramazani was interrupted by the arrival of an IRGC lieutenant. He was handed a folder labeled "*Kheili Seri*" (TOP SECRET) on the outside. Underneath, the phrase "extremely urgent" was written in red.

After reading several lines, Colonel Ramazani turned to Massoud. "There is an urgent matter that requires my attention. I want to thank you for coming forward with this information. Get some rest. I'll contact you shortly to get more details about everyone involved."

Colonel Ramazani and his guest left the room without shaking his hand. Massoud wondered if he had done the right thing.

◆ ◆ ◆

The Samsung big screen displayed a scene from the classic movie *Scarface*. Inside his eleventh floor condominium, Massoud rested on a plush leather sofa as he ate pizza. It was Friday, the day of rest and prayer. His smartphone suddenly came to life. He didn't recognize the number.

"Hello?"

"Massoud, meet me in front of your building in fifteen minutes."

"Yes, sir, but—" The caller hung up before he could finish. It was a bit odd that of all days, Colonel Ramazani had chosen Friday to conduct this business. Massoud changed his clothes and took the elevators downstairs. The pizza and the Al Pacino movie would have to wait. Colonel Ramazani arrived in a BMW sedan in front of his building. Behind the wheel was a herculean driver. As he opened the door to the back seat, Hassan Hashemi was already seated. Massoud wished he could have finished his food. Perhaps he could return in time for dinner. After several minutes, Massoud spoke out, "Colonel, this is not the way to IRGC-IO Headquarters."

It was silent as the colonel and Hassan stared out their respective windows. The sign for Evin Prison indicated that something was not quite right.

"Why are we here?" The only sound in the car was the heavy pounding of his heart. They pulled through the gate into the courtyard. Hassan got out and walked over to the other side to open the door for Massoud.

"Step out of the vehicle and follow me," Hassan said.

Massoud hesitated briefly before complying.

"Turn around and face the wall," Hassan ordered.

As soon as Massoud turned, he was blindfolded and cuffed. Someone pulled on his chain as he was led for several minutes, going up and down a flight of stairs, then up some more stairs. A door creaked, and he was dragged inside. The moldy scent and frigid air were unwelcoming. He sensed there were no windows in this room. He was pushed into a chair from behind. The blindfold was removed. He was sitting across Hassan. Colonel Ramazani was holding a folder in the distance.

"Where am I?"

"Section 2A of Evin Prison," Hassan said.

His mouth became dry; he tried to maintain his composure. Asghar must have dug up some incriminating information in Kuala Lumpur.

"Can you please tell me why I'm here? I came forward to help the IRGC-IO uncover a coup against the supreme leader. Is this the than—" His face stung as a loud slap reverberated through the room.

"We'll do the talking around here. Your only job is to answer." Hassan barked.

His mouth replied reflexively before his mind had the chance to make another mistake. "Yes, sir!"

"Who was the man you met the night Javad came to visit in Kuala Lumpur?" Hassan said.

"What man?"

He had not finished saying the word "man" before a heavy fist knocked him out of his chair. He was promptly picked up and put back in place.

"The American that came to your room. The one whose friends showed up later that evening with a large suitcase."

How could they have known? He hadn't told anyone. *Wop*! A wooden ruler struck his face and broke. The pieces fell to the floor before he could scream out in agony.

"Who was the man in your room that night in Kuala Lumpur? Give some thought to your answer. Your body can't afford another wrong reply," Hassan warned.

"What are you talking about?" Massoud said.

Hassan stood over him now. The interrogator turned to Colonel Ramazani who moved his head up and down. Hassan walked out of the room, closing the door behind him. Massoud was still hazy from the beating. He was determined not to reveal his contact with the American. There was no way he would be allowed to continue his involvement with the missile program if they knew the truth. He was an accomplice in the murder of an IRGC intelligence officer. He was certain they were bluffing.

Hassan returned with an electric generator connected to several cables. If these men were bluffing, they were good at it. Colonel Ramazani approached him and said, "If you've not figured it out by now, Hassan is an expert on making people talk. He's the best in the business. The only time he fails is when someone chooses to die instead of talk."

The colonel stepped out of the way, motioning Hassan to hurry along. The interrogator was as cool as a cucumber. He methodically set up his instruments on a small table, adjusting them one by one.

"I'm going to ease you into this gently so you don't pass out," Hassan said.

Colonel Ramazani moved behind his chair to hold him in place while Hassan pulled his pants down. The interrogator calmly attached two freezing clasps onto his testicles. The clasps were each attached to an electric wire. Hassan flipped a switch before putting his hand on a knob.

"Who was the man that came to your room the night Javad Pirnia disappeared?" After twenty seconds of silence, the distinct sounds of electricity shot through his ears. The sound was immediately drowned out by his own horrendous scream. He had no idea he could yell that loud. The pain in his throat was probably the result of a torn vocal cord.

"Are you going to talk, or should I make some scrambled eggs?" Hassan said. At least another minute went by, maybe more, before the knob turned once again.

"Aaaaaaaaaaaagh!" Massoud screamed.

The distinct aroma of burning flesh permeated the room. It was so bad that Colonel Ramazani ran out while vomiting. Hassan didn't share the colonel's predicament; it was definitely not his first time doing this. The sadistic interrogator was enjoying every second. Massoud could only imagine how intoxicating having all that power over a man could be. His body was drained of energy. He no longer had the will to resist.

"Please make it stop. I'll tell you everything, please make the pain go away!" Massoud begged as he wept uncontrollably.

Hassan walked toward the door and shouted out into the hallway. "Colonel, please come inside. Massoud has something to tell you."

Colonel Ramazani walked back in, still visibly shaken. He was wearing a mask, probably to block the scent of Massoud's burning testicles.

"The man in my room was a CIA officer. His name was John King. He was at the hotel to ask me about our missile program."

"How did he know about our program?" Colonel Ramazani said.

"I approached the American Embassy in Kuala Lumpur. I was upset about being passed over for a promotion. I decided to get revenge and make some money to alleviate my anger."

"So you sold out your country for selfish reasons?" Colonel Ramazani said.

"Yes" Massoud groaned.

"What happened to Javad Pirnia?" Colonel Ramazani asked.

"I was not expecting him to be at the hotel that night. He knocked on the door, and I let him in. He then proceeded to tell me that he was going to report the incident. Suddenly, the American came out of his hiding place in the closet. After a brief struggle, the American killed Javad. He then called his colleagues, who came by and took Javad's body in a suitcase."

"Now we're getting somewhere. I knew most of these facts already after reading a report filed by my men in Singapore. They bribed an employee of the Grand Hyatt Hotel in

Kuala Lumpur to turn over the surveillance video from the night in question. We knew Javad disappeared in your room. I just needed an explanation as to what happened. I suspected that your American contact was a CIA man."

"What are you going to do to me?"

"This country does not need any more traitors. I don't care how educated you are. We can always train more people to replace you!" Colonel Ramazani turned to Hassan, "Have your fun with this piece of garbage, then send him to hell."

"Please, *nooooooo!*" Massoud screamed. Colonel Ramazani ran out as quickly as possible.

47. PORT KHALID, SHARJAH, UAE

November 25

T he Chengdu, a cargo ship, arrived an hour early. It was carrying hazardous material to the Canton Trading warehouse at the Port of Sharjah, UAE. The ship measured approximately one hundred twenty feet from bow to stern. Registered in Singapore, it was the property of Canton Trading. Eight crewmembers, including Mr. Chen, began unloading the cargo. It took forty-five minutes to transport the containers to the warehouse. Mr. Chen's cell phone rang. It was the CEO of Gulf Limited LLC.

"Hello?"

"It's Farzad, how much longer?" The caller said as Mr. Chen put him on speaker.

"Your cargo is ready. Come by anytime." Mr. Chen said.

"I'll send a few of my men right over. We're bringing our own equipment, so please inform your security."

"No problem." Mr. Chen turned to Janusz. He was holding a briefcase.

"I believe once this transaction is complete, Canton Trading will have fulfilled its obligations to Rostami Partners. We just need—"

"Your money is right here," Janusz said, pointing to the briefcase.

He was standing next to Eric who had accompanied him in case there was trouble. Everything was going according to the plan, but Janusz still had butterflies in his stomach. What if the cargo exploded prematurely? What if the IRGC found out

they were being played? The zealots in Tehran were not de-
terred by a nuclear holocaust. All they wanted was to cause
maximum devastation to hasten the return of Imam Mahdi.

An elite six-man commando team of hostage rescue operators from the Iranian regular army's 65th Airborne Brigade
was ready to take down the warehouse. They had orders to kill
everyone inside the building. The supreme leader had personally requested them for this mission. They were the most highly
trained team in Iran. Even the IRGC didn't have any units trained
to the same level of proficiency as the 65th Airborne Hostage
Rescue Team.

Each man on the team had been promised a hundred
thousand dollars as a bonus for a successful operation. The
motorcycle mounted men rode into a cargo container attached
to an eighteen-wheel truck. They were waived through the
main gate, promptly heading to the warehouse. They saw their
driver wave to a man on their wristwatch display. Someone was
driving a forklift loaded with barrels toward their truck.

They waited for the rear doors to open. A man was shouting outside, "Are you going to open the cargo door?"

"Of course, don't worry!" the driver said.

The driver pointed his Uzi and opened fire. They watched
as a man's face was riddled with bullets causing an immediate
splattering of blood and brain matter. The cargo doors suddenly swung open as they flew out one by one. Two of them
surrounded the forklift operator. They expertly opened fire,
making sure to avoid the explosive barrels on the front. The remaining four motorcycles rode quickly through the warehouse,
shooting anything that moved. Within minutes, they had elim-
inated everyone they could find. They were still not satisfied.
The team leader spoke into the headset.

"Have you found the American?"

"Not yet, sir."

"What are you waiting for?"

Janusz and Eric witnessed the unfolding scene from the far end of the warehouse. "Eric, what the fuck is going on? Why are the Iranians shooting?"

"They must have been tipped off. How is that possible?"

"It makes no difference now. If we don't get these guys, we're going home in body bags."

"I only have a pistol with an extra magazine," Eric said.

"I'm in the same boat. Let's split up; otherwise, the motorcycles will cut us down before we can run out of here."

"How many are there?" Eric asked.

"At least six on the bikes plus two in the truck."

"Fuck, they're headed this way. Good luck, Janusz!"

They each took cover behind stacks of boxes inside the warehouse. The motorcycles rode through like the Mongol horde. They knocked down shelves and stacks to ferret them out. It was only a matter of time. Janusz noticed he had a good shot at the rider closest to his position. He took aim and fired—*bang*! A direct hit. The rider went down. Two more bikes raced toward Janusz's position. He'd be lucky to get one before the other opened up with his Uzi. At least there would be one fewer for Eric to fight off. The roar of the engines was getting closer. He counted down in his head. *Five, four, three, two.... pop, pop.* Eric bolted out of nowhere and fired at the lead bike. The driver went down. Eric then fired at another bike. *Pop! Pop! Pop!*

The third driver also went down. Eric did not see the fourth bike that made a pincer move to his side. As Janusz watched the scene unfold, the fourth driver let loose a fusillade that riddled Eric's body. It was too late to do anything other than to take aim. Janusz immediately fired twice. *Bang, Bang,* both shots found their mark. Janusz arrived as Eric gasped for air. He knelt to hold Eric's hand. How could he have let this happen? Eric stared at him as he spat out blood. His eyes seemed distant. Perhaps his thoughts were with his son and daughter in Australia. He would never see them grow up; he would never go to their weddings. There was only one thing left to say.

"Don't worry Eric, I'll look after them. Your wife, your kids, I'll help any way I can." Eric tightened his grip around his hand. Blood poured out of his mouth as he stopped breathing. His body went limp and his eyes were frozen. His head slumped to the side. Janusz assessed the situation. Four of the six bikes were out of commission, but Janusz wanted revenge. He quickly ran toward the nearest abandoned bike. He grabbed the Uzi next to it. The scalding muzzle seared his inattentive fingers.

The team leader at the other end of the warehouse was ready to move. Using the headset, he quickly relayed his orders to the remaining men.

"Four down. Place the cargo in the truck and let's roll."

The driver jumped out to maneuver the forklift inside his truck. The leader requested guidance from the nearby command base.

"Team lead to base, team lead to base. We have four men down. Unable to kill all targets. What are your instructions?"

"Team lead, this is base. Escort the cargo to the ship immediately. Blow up the warehouse and get back out to international waters. Do you copy?"

"Roger!"

Janusz revved the engine, ready to charge the Iranian assassins at full speed. He was neither rational nor concerned about his own safety. As he closed in, a mounted assassin let loose a hail of bullets that tore through his front tire. He tried to keep the bike steady but given his speed, it was no use. Janusz slid twenty feet across the floor on his back. There was a sharp pain in his right leg and a stinging burn in his left arm. He could barely move. He was helpless to stop the escape of the retreating motorcycles. They escorted the eighteen-wheeler out of the warehouse as he tried to get back up.

The team leader pushed his bike past one hundred kilometers per hour. He was ready to shoot at any obstacle in his path. To his surprise, the gate guards had disappeared. They raced out of the Canton Trading facility without encountering resistance.

When they reached their docks, the IRGC's foremen expeditiously loaded the precious cargo. Their ship was out of port within fifteen minutes. The men on deck had rocket launchers and heavy-caliber machine guns. It was soon apparent that a firefight would not be necessary. The warehouse exploded at exactly the same time as the IRGC ship left port. Not long after, they were in international waters. Those bonuses were well deserved.

48. BURJ-AL-KHALIFAH, DUBAI, UAE

November 27

T wo days after the explosion in Sharjah, Tony's office phone rang at 8:35 a.m. He picked up as soon as he walked in.

"It was a setup. They knew we were coming."

"Janusz, thank God. We thought you were dead. What the fuck happened out there?"

"The Iranians were tipped off."

"Jesus!"

"We were greeted by a Special Forces hit team. They were good, even by our standards. I'm betting they were with the 65th Airborne Brigade, the NOHED. They—" Janusz paused. "They got Eric."

"Fuck, I bet it was Canton Trading. They must have sold us out," Tony said.

"No, I don't think so. They had every incentive to keep their mouths shut. Anyway, the Iranians killed them too, including Mr. Chen. I was the only one who survived."

"What took you so long to call?"

"I was shot. I barely escaped before they blew up the warehouse. I called the doctor you had set up for this mission. He took care of my wounds and brought me to the safe house in the Burj Khalifa. I'm still in bed, and I feel like shit."

"You need anything?"

"No, the place is fully stocked. I just need another day or two to recover."

"Take your time. You can come back when you're ready.

The shit has really hit the fan this time."

"That's the least of our problems," Janusz said.

"What do you mean?"

"As we speak, all elements of the IRGC missile program are on maximum alert. We may wake up one morning to the sounds of an incoming Iranian nuclear attack."

"What do you suggest?"

"We don't have any attractive options. We should inform the SSCI so they can warn the president," Janusz said.

"That could mean acknowledging the existence of the Unit. The civil liberties groups are going to call for a full investigation and ask for our heads."

"Yes, but the president can order an immediate strike against all suspected Iranian nuclear and missile facilities."

"What happened to the fuel?"

"The Iranians took it with them."

"Why would they do that if they were tipped off?"

"Beats the fuck out of me. Perhaps they'll sell it to someone else, or maybe they plan to use it despite the risk. Whatever the reason, I don't particularly care."

"I know you're angry about Eric."

"That's an understatement. I do have one request."

"What is it?"

"Let me go back to finish the job. I want another shot at this. We can't allow the Hojjatieh to get what they want."

"Are you out of your fucking mind? You just said yourself that all the officials tied to the program are under protection. You're lucky they didn't kill you the last time."

"Tony, we have no other choice. This was my fuck-up, and I want to fix it."

"Out of the fucking question. We're not going to do anything until we figure out what went wrong. You're talking out of your ass, probably because of the painkillers."

"Tony—"

"Listen to me very carefully. Just hang on and wait until I tell you what your next move will be."

The Meydan Racecourse was one of the largest and most beautiful venues of its kind in the world. The sixty-thousand-seat capacity horse track in Dubai was a favorite hangout of the local elite. They came to see and to be seen. In contrast to the others, Janusz did not want to be recognized. Having missed his chance to kill Dr. Esfehani, he was in desperate need of an outlet. At times like these, he was overtaken by an uncontrollable urge to play the odds. He was not familiar with any of the horses or their jockeys. As luck would have it, he'd somehow salvaged the suitcase containing the last installment of funds for Mr. Chen.

There was exactly one million dollars in cash that Mr. Chen had requested to be delivered in a briefcase. Janusz wired the money to a betting account he maintained in Las Vegas. Perhaps the unlucky Mr. Chen had similar plans for the cash. Either way, the deceased former chief executive of Canton Trading no longer had any use for the money. Tony hadn't asked about it either, probably assuming the money had evaporated during the explosion in Sharjah. For the first time in his life, Janusz was going to gamble to his heart's content.

He bet large sums with the bookies back in Vegas. Gambling was illegal in Dubai, but the Vegas bookies were able to follow the action on satellite TV. After everything that had happened, he was entitled to this moment. He was determined to lose the entire sum of cash tonight as if his life depended on it. In some strange way, it did. It was the perfect opportunity to get gambling out of his system before he proposed to Jennifer.

49. TEHRAN, IRAN AND HERNDON, VA

November 29

I t was a beautiful morning in Tehran. The birds were chirping, and the air was crisp. There was none of the dreaded air pollution. Street vendors sold everything from pistachios to barbecued corn on the cob. Then it happened. At first, it seemed like an earthquake. Reports of the shockwave came from all over the city. Perhaps the Americans had finally struck preemptively. An eerie silence fell over the capital as everyone tried to find out what it was that shook the ground with such terrible force.

After canceling their scheduled broadcasts, the local authorities made a public announcement. They claimed there had been a dreadful accident in the suburb of Malard, west of the capital. The explosion had occurred at an IRGC arms depot. According to the Iranian Government, an accidental fire had detonated the bombs at an armory. Two hours later, it was reported that at least forty IRGC personnel at the facility had been killed. Among them was a man most Iranians had never heard of. He was remembered as Dr. Abbas Esfehani Moghaddas. The announcement claimed that Dr. Esfehani was the father of Iran's missile program.

The broadcast stated the supreme leader would attend Dr. Esfehani's funeral, scheduled to take place a few days later. Amid the confusion, a local newspaper had sent a reporter to visit Dr. Esfehani's brother, Amir Esfehani. He too was an officer in the IRGC. Amir Esfehani initially claimed that his brother had been working on a secret missile project for the IRGC. According to Amir, his brother had been killed during the testing phase of a fuel for an indigenous ICBM intended to attack the United States. Iranian authorities immediately denied the story. They claimed Amir had been so distraught by his brother's death that he was confused. Amir subsequently denied making the statement to the media. The international press corps was much more excited about the story. The foreign pundits had all kinds of theories. Most speculated that the world had just witnessed a preemptive strike on Iran's nuclear program.

Janusz stood in Stan's office on the sixth floor. He had decided to return and jump back to work. A strategy meeting was scheduled for that afternoon. He was in the middle of a conversation when Stan turned to Fox News.

"Hey, hold up. Hold up. Turn up the sound," Janusz said.

"What the fuck! I wonder what that's all about?" Stan said.

"Hey, this is at Malard. There are no nuclear facilities there. Jesus, the missile facility just blew up," Janusz said. The news of Dr. Esfehani's death came as a surprise.

"Stan, get Tony in here now," Janusz said. After a few minutes, Tony joined the group in front of the TV.

"Tony, I'm not sure what happened, but our mission was a success after all," Janusz said.

They sat around the TV for the next few hours desperately waiting to learn more. It was sad that the media was, for the moment, a better source of information on this event than the American intelligence community.

"I wonder what happened to the coup plotters," Janusz said.

"Why don't you contact your source in Tehran?" Stan said. They were glued to the TV late into the evening. The more theories they came up with, the more questions needed answers. Without solid intelligence on the ground, there was no way to be certain.

50. OFFICE OF SUPREME LEADER MASHHADI, CENTRAL TEHRAN, IRAN

November 29

Ayatollah Mashhadi sat in his garden enjoying the sounds of nature. He was disappointed the grounds keepers had not planted more red flowers. The color red symbolized the blood of martyrs. Without blood, there would have been no revolution. It was blood that kept the revolution alive all these years. *Where did you come from?* A white butterfly landed on one of his Chrysanthemums. The supreme leader sucked on his pipe as his mind wandered. How nice it would be if every now and then he could transform himself into a butterfly. He could then roam freely through endless fields of flowers without a care in the world. These butterflies were lucky not to be burdened with the responsibilities of power. Without warning, Katkhodah Lankarani stormed into his garden sanctuary. The director of the IRGC-IO walked rapidly and with purpose.

"Sir, I come bearing great news."

"Katkhodah, do you ever observe the butterflies in envy of how carefree their lives appear?"

"I don't have the luxury of such thoughts, sir. I'm too busy trying to protect us from threats against the regime."

"What can I do for you on this lovely day?"

"I thought you'd be happy to know that Dr. Esfehani and his traitorous colleagues have departed this earth for the gates of hell."

"Thanks to Allah, my ears are still able to hear the explosion that shook the city today."

"I also wanted to relay that the IRGC-IO has placed Generals Jafarzadeh, Vatanparast, and Javadpoor under arrest, along with Admiral Abbasi, Yadollah Boroujerdi, and President Azari. We're about to fully drain the cesspool of sedition that's infected our regime," Katkhodah said.

"There is one thing that still confuses me."

"What's that, sir?"

"How did you find out that the shipment headed for the missile program had been compromised?"

"I give full credit to my men. When one of them went missing in Kuala Lumpur, we received a call from Massoud that an American had approached him. I sent two more men to Malaysia to follow up. It didn't take long to find the American and his hiding place. Our surveillance revealed that the American was headed to Iceland to talk to an arms dealer about our missile program."

"I may have underestimated you."

"We killed the American's contact in Iceland, but unfortunately, he escaped that time. We were also monitoring Mr. Chen, the Chinese executive, who agreed to supply Massoud with fuel for our ICBM. A carefully placed bug in Mr. Chen's vehicle revealed that he had received an offer from an Iranian company based in UAE by the name of Rostami Partners. We suspected that Rostami Partners was a CIA front used to infiltrate our procurement network. Our suspicions were confirmed when our surveillance of the American safe house in Kuala Lumpur revealed that two of their operatives were headed to Sharjah. We decided to teach the Americans a lesson by eliminating them along with their lackeys in Canton Trading. We then dealt with the treasonous Dr. Esfehani by allowing the tainted fuel to reach his team, resulting in the explosion you heard this morning. I'm happy to report that all elements involved in this treachery have been neutralized." Katkhodah said.

"What about the American who infiltrated our program?

Did you get him too?"

"Of course, he was killed along with the others as I just told you."

"Katkhodah, you forget I have eyes and ears at every level of this government."

"What do you mean, sir?"

"For example, a cousin of mine works directly for you. Colonel Ramazani tells a different version of this story."

Katkhodah's face turned white. He was blindsided by the supreme leader's revelation.

"My cousin says that he was the one who ordered the surveillance of Massoud over your objections. He also tells me that the 65th Airborne was unable to eliminate everyone at the Sharjah warehouse."

For the first time in as long as Ayatollah Mashhadi could remember, Katkhodah had no reply.

"You've forgotten that your number one priority is to ensure the safety of this regime while being truthful with me. Since you've disturbed my tranquility with half-truths and trivialities, you should turn yourself over to the *Vali-e Amr* guards on your way out. Colonel Ramazani will help me decide your fate. If you don't mind, I'll get back to my flowers and butterflies."

51. UNIT 81 HEADQUARTERS, HERNDON, VA

November 30

J anusz spent the entire morning in Tony's office poring over intelligence reports related to the explosion. They were eager to learn how the IRGC had become suspicious of the Canton Trading propellant deal. The bigger question was why the tainted fuel was delivered to Dr. Esfehani's team. Something didn't add up. The puzzle had too many missing pieces.

"One thing is clear amid all this," Tony said.

"What's that?"

"We need to get rid of the evidence tying us to this mess. The warehouse in Sharjah can easily be tied back to us. It's safe to assume the IRGC has connected the dots between Rostami, Canton Trading, and HRC."

"Yes and no. We purchased Rostami Partners using a shell company registered in Belgium. The IRGC won't be able to connect the dots back to us. They'll assume the CIA purchased Rostami Partners. Anyway, we've already dissolved Rostami Partners."

Tony walked over to the far side of the room to retrieve a secure incoming fax. Five minutes later, he was giddy with excitement.

"Janusz, you should read this."

"Read what?"

"Jason Osborne just sent it in. It's a CIA analysis of the explosion in Malard. You're not going to believe it!"

Janusz took the document. The assessment was based on raw reports from a source present at the meetings in addition to the intercepted emails from the supreme leader's office. The summary of the report read as follows:

TOP SECRET

UPON RECEIVING INFORMATION FROM SINGAPORE THAT A CIA OPERATIVE HAD INFILTRATED THE IRGC's PROCUREMENT NETWORK, THE SUPREME LEADER ORDERED A HIT TEAM TO KILL EVERYONE ASSOCIATED WITH CANTON TRADING AND DEVELOPMENT LLC. SUBSEQUENTLY, COLONEL RAMAZANI INFORMED THE SUPREME LEADER THAT THE FUEL DR. ES-FEHANI'S TEAM HAD PURCHASED WAS LIKELY SABOTAGED. COLONEL RAMAZANI THEN ADVISED THE SUPREME LEADER THAT IN LIGHT OF THE EARLIER REVELATIONS THAT DR. ESFEHANI AND MEMBERS OF HIS TEAM WERE PARTICIPANTS IN A PLANNED COUP, WHICH INCLUDED A PREEMPTIVE NU-CLEAR STRIKE AGAINST THE UNITED STATES, THEY COULD SOLVE BOTH PROBLEMS BY ALLOWING THE TAINTED FUEL TO REACH DR. ESFEHANI. THIS ACTION WOULD ELIMINATE THE TRAITOROUS SCIENTIST AS A THREAT AGAINST THE REGIME AND AVERT A WAR WITH THE UNITED STATES. FOL-LOWING THE EXPLOSION AT MALARD, PRESIDENT AZARI AND HIS ACCOMPLICES WERE ARRESTED AND CHARGED WITH EMBEZZLEMENT. THEY WILL BE SENTENCED SHORTLY. THE SUPREME LEADER PERSONALLY APPROVED THESE ACTIONS. DESPITE THE INEVITABLE DELAY IN THE BURAQ ICBM PRO-GRAM, IT APPEARS THAT THE PRESERVATION OF THE REGIME WAS MORE IMPORTANT THAN OTHER CONSIDERATIONS.

TOP SECRET

"Son of a bitch! They knew exactly what we wanted to do, yet they let it happen. Dr. Esfehani's plan to eliminate Ayatollah Mashhadi was a sin they could not forgive. They calculated that it would be better if he were dead!" Janusz said.

"I guess you were wrong."

"About what?"

"You didn't fail. Your sabotage plan gave them the perfect opportunity to eliminate Dr. Esfehani. Without your initiative, none of this would've happened."

"That's one way to look at it," Janusz said.

"Janusz."

"What?"

"You were wrong about something else."

"Go on."

"Ayatollah Mashhadi's biggest fear is not the United States. For the supreme leader, in particular, his survival is the overriding factor. Heaven help us if the Hojjatieh is able to replace him with someone truly determined to bring back Imam Mahdi."

"No doubt. Especially since the next time they may have a nuclear-tipped ICBM!" The weight of the world suddenly lifted off Janusz's shoulders. His country was safe, at least for the time being.

Janusz went back to his own office to let the events of the past few weeks sink in. Before he reached the elevator, he remembered that he needed some time to tend to another matter.

52. VINEYARD NEAR THE HOME OF THOMAS JEFFERSON, CHARLOTTESVILLE, VA

The Following April

I t was a sunny day in central Virginia. The trees were green, and the flowers were full of colors. Janusz was quite fond of the dogwoods, especially the white ones. Then again, his eyes never got tired of gazing at the purple on the Avondale Redbuds. The flowers were even more vivid than he remembered them from years past. Janusz and Jennifer had always enjoyed driving through this part of the country. They had spent many summers visiting the local wineries that dotted the landscape. It was only fitting to have their wedding at a winery near Thomas Jefferson's Monticello. This particular location was filled with memories, including their first kiss. It had happened after tasting a pairing of white wine with chocolate truffle.

The guest list included their closest friends and relatives. They treated the guests to a weekend wedding that began Friday night and ended Sunday afternoon. Jennifer's parents flew in from Minnesota.

After losing a million dollars in one night, Janusz was certain that he'd finally kicked the urge to gamble. He was even seeing an addiction specialist. Fifteen minutes before the ceremony, Janusz grabbed his father's arm and pulled him aside for a stroll through one of the tree-lined gardens on the estate.

"I want you to know something before I exchange my vows," Janusz said.

"Yes?"

"I'm eternally grateful that you and Mom decided to stay here after the Iranian Revolution. I recently had the opportunity to visit the old country on a business trip. It's as beautiful as you've said, but those in charge are quite evil. Without getting into details, I provided some payback to the regime for what they did to Ben. It doesn't replace our loss, but at least justice was done. Along the way, I may have made the future safer for all Americans."

"Why are you telling me this?"

"Because you've impacted my life in more ways than you can imagine. Jennifer and I chose this place for a variety of reasons. Suffice it to say that the historical connection to Thomas Jefferson was one of them. I believe men like Jefferson have continued in the footsteps of Cyrus the Great. I realize more than ever now that the American constitution written way back in 1787 represents a set of ideas worth dying for. Thank you for all the sacrifices you made on my behalf. I'm sure it hasn't been easy, especially after I started gambling. I'm truly happy with my life on this day."

His father wiped away the tears and kissed Janusz on both cheeks.

"Son, I've never been more proud of you. Thank you for whatever it is that you did on behalf of your brother and your country. Ben would have also been proud of you if he'd been here today. I'm sure he's looking down on us with a smile right now. Come, let's make this marvelous day official."

Janusz and Jennifer exchanged their vows under a picture-perfect sunset. It was a moment that may have never happened if President Azari and Dr. Esfehani had prevailed. As the newly-weds made their way down the aisle, Janusz and Tony locked eyes ever so briefly. They both understood that the demise of the Hojjatieh would not end the threat from Iran. The work of the Unit against Iran's terrorist regime was just beginning.

THE END

GLOSSARY OF TERMS AND NAMES

Admiral Ali-Reza Abbasi: Iranian Defense Minister.

Aerospace Industries Organization (AIO): A state-run company within the Iranian Ministry of Defense responsible for the production of missiles for both the IRGC and the Artesh.

Allies Bank of Singapore: The official bank of Canton Trading.

Asghar Tavakoli: IRGC-IO officer working the Javad Pirnia disappearance case.

Ayatollah Mashhadi: Current supreme leader of Iran.

Ayatollah Semnani: Father of the Iranian Revolution and architect of the system of Velayat-e Faqih.

Ben Soltani: Janusz's younger brother.

Canton Trading Company: A company owned by Chinese nationals operating in Singapore. Canton Trading procures weapons systems from China's military.

Defense Industries Organization (DIO): A state-run company within the Iranian Ministry of Defense responsible for weapons production for the land forces of both the IRGC and regular Iranian military (Artesh).

Donald Patrick: Chairman of the Senate Select Committee on Intelligence (SSCI).

Dr. Nathan Anderson: Missile propulsion expert working for the Unit.

Dr. Pavel Yevchenko: Lead Russian scientist for the IRGC's nuclear weapons program.

Ed Wright: The Unit's technical and surveillance expert.

Eric Bradford: Former CIA officer and operative for the Unit.

Evin Prison: Iran's main institution for holding political prisoners. Evin has separate wards run by the MOIS (section 209) and the IRGC-IO (section 2A).

Farhad Soltani: Janusz's father.

Farzad Gilani: Businessman who establishes front companies for the IRGC in countries with no ties to Iran.

First Australia Bank: The official bank of the Unit's front in Australia, The Oceana Company.

Gulf Limited LLC: A front company set up in Dubai by Farzad Gilani to provide cover for the IRGC missile procurement team in Malaysia and Singapore.

Colonel Hadi Ramazani: IRGC Intelligence Organization deputy in charge of ferreting out "deviants" within the Iranian regime.

Hamid Azari-Tabar: President of the Islamic Republic of Iran.

Hojjatieh Society: Underground messianic sect plotting to hasten the return of the hidden 12th Imam.

Imam Hussein University: The IRGC's university with both graduate and undergraduate programs.

IRGC Aerospace Forces: A branch of the IRGC with an air force, a unit that operates UAV's, air defense units, and Iran's missile forces.

IRGC Ansar al Mahdi Personal Protection Unit: IRGC unit tasked with the protection of senior government officials and VIPs.

IRGC Intelligence Organization (IRGC-IO): The Intelligence arm of the IRGC.

IRGC Missile Command Headquarters: The IRGC Missile Command Headquarters maintains operational control of Iran's ballistic missiles.

IRGC Qods Force (QF): Branch of the IRGC with the mission to support and train Iran's foreign proxies and to carry out intelligence operations outside Iran's borders.

IRGC Vali-e Amr Unit: IRGC unit specifically tasked with protecting the Supreme Leader.

Islamic Revolutionary Guard Corps (IRGC): A branch of the Iranian military founded after the Islamic revolution to safeguard the new regime.

James Black: The Unit's technical expert on polygraphs.

Janusz Soltani: The Unit's top operative for the Middle East.

Jason Osborne: SSCI senior staffer/intelligence analyst who liaises with the Unit.

Javad Pirnia: IRGC-IO officer reporting to Colonel Ramazani. Javad was responsible for the security of the missile procurement team in Malaysia.

Jennifer Odenhagen: Janusz's girlfriend.

Johan Olafsson: Arms dealer in Akureyri, Iceland.

Katkhodah Lankarani: Director of the IRGC-IO.

Lavizan: Wealthy neighborhood in Northern Tehran where high-ranking officers of the IRGC live.

Malard Missile Research Facility: IRGC facility west of Tehran where most of the Research & Development for the Iranian long-range ballistic missile program occurs.

Massoud Hosseinzadeh: The Director's protégé and head of missile procurement team in Malaysia and Singapore.

Ministry of Intelligence (MOIS): Iranian civilian intelligence agency.

Mohsen Jafarzadeh: IRGC Commander and member of the Hojjatieh.

Mojtaba Vatanparast: IRGC Aerospace Forces Commander and member of the Hojjatieh.

Mr. Chen: Head of Canton Trading Company.

NAJA: Acronym for Iranian Police.

Parchin Armaments Complex: Military Research facility where Iranian military conducts research on both nuclear weapons and ballistic missiles.

Pars Aluminum: Company with which Janusz Soltani (Ian Phillips) conducts business in Tehran as a cover for his mission.

Paulina Soltani: Janusz's mother.

Political Ideological Directorate: Embedded at every level of all Iranian military and security units, the PID is in charge of indoctrinating military personnel with Islamic values in support of the supreme leader. This organization is run by clerics trained at Shahid Mahallati University.

General Reza Zanjani: IRGC Brigadier General and a member of the Hojjatieh. Reza Zanjani is Janusz's source in Tehran.

Rostami Partners: An import-export company registered in Dubai that is purchased by the Unit for access to Iran.

Saman Shooshtari: IRGC-IO officer working the Javad Pirnia disappearance case with his partner Asghar Tavakoli.

Stan Roth: Tony Volpe's deputy in charge of the Unit.

The Director: Top engineer and Director of the IRGC's long-range missile program.

The Oceana Company: Australian private equity firm set up by the Unit to allow its members to travel to countries hostile to the US.

Tom Stone: Head of research and analysis at the Unit.

Tony Volpe: CEO of High Risk Capital (HRC) and Director of the Unit.

Unit 81/High Risk Capital (HRC): Unit 81, known as the Unit, is a private intelligence agency established in 1981. HRC is a private equity firm that serves as the cover for Unit 81. HRC is located in Herndon, VA.

Velayat-e Faqih: System of government where an Islamic Jurist (senior cleric) is the most powerful individual in charge of society as both commander-in-chief of the military and final arbiter of all domestic and foreign policy.

Yadollah Boroujerdi: Director of the Political Ideological Directorate of the Armed Forces General Staff.

101 Collins Street: A 57 floor Melbourne high-rise where the Unit maintains condo's, offices, and conference rooms. The Unit owns floors 30 to 33 in this building.

IF YOU ENJOYED THIS STORY, PLEASE PROVIDE A REVIEW ON AMAZON